Kyle's never been shy about going after what he wants. After two short term contracts, he wants something closer to permanent with Aidan. And what better way to bring them closer than to spend time apart? Being away from each other for the first time in their relationship might make them both realize they'd rather be together.

TO LOVE AND TO CHERISH

Enchanting Encounters, Book Three

Tamryn Eradani

A NineStar Press Publication

Published by NineStar Press
P.O. Box 91792,
Albuquerque, New Mexico, 87199 USA.
www.ninestarpress.com

To Love and to Cherish

Printed in the USA
First Edition
May, 2019

Print ISBN: 978-1-950412-70-9

Also available in eBook, ISBN: 978-1-950412-68-6

Chapter One

MUSIC FILTERS THROUGH the speakers of the dance club, this song less deafening than the last. The singer's voice is lower, crooning, and every beat of the bass reverberates through Kyle's body. He moves with the music, chasing it, his movements too languid to ever completely catch it.

The guy behind him groans as Kyle grinds back against him. He splays his hands across Kyle's hips and pulls Kyle back against him, as if there's any space left between them at this point.

"You're good at this," the guy says, his breath hot against Kyle's ear.

Kyle grins as he tips his head back against the guy's shoulder. It shows off the long line of his throat, even in the dim lighting of the club. It's a tease, all that skin, shiny with a sheen of sweat, more than Kyle meant it to be. The guy tightens his hold as he dips his lips to Kyle's neck.

"Makes me wonder what else you're good at," the guy says.

Yep, definitely too much of a tease. Kyle stops the man's hands from creeping up his shirt.

"Tonight, just dancing," Kyle tells the stranger.

"I could persuade you." He dips his thumbs into Kyle's waistband. It's his turn to grind against Kyle, and Kyle's honest enough to admit the man's packing a pretty persuasive argument.

It's tempting, but he has someone even better waiting for him tonight.

"You can't," Kyle says, apologetic as he turns so they're face to face.

The guy's a couple of inches taller than Kyle, but he doesn't make him feel small. He likes a bit of looming from his partners, and he's met some people who pull it off even though they're shorter than him, but this guy doesn't manage it even with a natural advantage. It's a good reminder that while this has been fun, this isn't the guy he wants to spend the rest of his night with.

The man's hands on are Kyle's ass now. They roamed during the past two songs, touching what seems like every part of Kyle's body. His skin is humming with it. He wants a harder touch, for them to slip under his clothes even though he just stopped the man from doing it.

Someone better is waiting for me at home.

It makes him wonder which of them he's really teasing.

Probably both.

"One more dance or no?" Kyle asks, his tone light so the guy knows there're no hard feelings either way.

"One more," the guy says.

He keeps Kyle like this, the two of them facing each other, as he draws him in closer. He's rougher during this song, because it has a faster beat or because he knows this is the last few minutes he has before Kyle disappears into the crowd.

Honestly, Kyle doesn't care what the reason is. He's into the hands that try to touch all of him one last time and the press of the guy's dick through his pants. He's really into the way the guy loses the rhythm of the music as if Kyle's more important than the dancing. By the end of the song, what they're doing can't be called dancing. Even with clothes on, it's borderline indecent.

Kyle unwraps himself from the other man and flashes him a thumbs-up before heading to the bar for a drink. He asks the bartender for lemonade because he's looking for a jolt of sugar.

He leans against the counter once he has his drink and looks out at the dance floor. It's hard to see more than shapes, just a mass of bodies writhing together. He takes a drink, the coldness of his lemonade a contrast to his overheated skin.

He checks his watch. He has to stay here for at least a half hour longer. Probably more. He doesn't want to seem too eager even though he *is* eager. All of this is to wind him up, and he's not sure how much more of it he can stand.

He takes another long drink before he holds his glass to his forehead. His face is flushed, and he's sweating. He'd worn one of his thinnest shirts in anticipation of a packed dance floor, and now it's plastered against his skin, it's practically see-through.

Once he finishes his drink, he leaves the cup and a tip for the bartender. There's a line for the bathroom, and by the time he's done, his clothes are sticky and uncomfortable from the sweat drying. Should he call it a night and head home? If he drives slowly enough, then he'll show up at the earliest time he was given. He was hoping to make it a little longer, but the teasing will be worth it.

A guy with spiked hair and a hopeful smile slides up to him. He's slimmer than Kyle and his cheeks are as pink as Kyle's feel. He has eyelashes that make Kyle jealous, and his shirt, if possible, clings even more than Kyle's is right now.

"You look like you're trying to have a good time," the guy says.

He isn't Kyle's type at all except he's interested, and that's Kyle's biggest turn on, more than eye color or body shape or gender. Maybe it makes him vain, but he finds himself leaning toward the other man.

"Not too good a time," Kyle cautions, because on a night like this, it's important he doesn't lead anyone on. Some guys assume he's playing hard to get, and those are the ones he cuts loose after a dance. He *is* looking for a good time, but his end game isn't anyone here.

The guy smiles, his teeth white and bright in the dark room. "That makes two of us."

Kyle shrugs and lets the guy lead him to a part of the dance floor he hasn't used yet tonight. It's on the edge, in full view of the bar. Kyle prefers being in the middle of things, bodies packed tight all around him.

It takes a whole song for him to realize the guy's looking over Kyle's shoulder toward the bar.

Their plans for the night really are the same.

Kyle hooks his fingers through the man's belt loops and tugs until he has his attention. "Do you have someone watching or someone you wish was watching?"

"Uh." The guy's gaze redirects to Kyle. He puts a few inches between them as if he's nervous. He must see something on Kyle's face that settles him because he says, "The first one."

Which means whoever it is must be sitting at the bar. Kyle wants to turn around and see for himself, but he holds off. First, he runs his hands through the guy's hair and tips his head back so they're looking at each other.

"What am I allowed to do?" Kyle asks.

He knows all about putting on a show. Getting people's attention is one of his best skills, and he's more than happy to help this guy have his good night.

The guy's eyebrows climb upwards. "You were definitely a good choice. You can do anything but kiss me."

"Anything? I can't kiss, but I can bite?"

"Not hard. No marks." His brow furrows. "Were you planning on it?"

"No, but you should be more careful offering blank checks to random guys you meet in dance clubs."

Warning issued, Kyle moves so his front is pressed to the guy's back and they're both facing the bar.

Being displayed is easily in Kyle's top five favorite positions to be in, and he plans on using that knowledge now. He leans in close so he can speak against the guy's ear. "Arms around my neck."

The guy obediently stretches his arms up and back so they're looped lightly around Kyle's neck. It opens up the guy's body, makes him one long line with nothing in the way. Kyle runs his hands down the guy's shirt and then rucks up the hem.

There's nothing subtle about what they're doing, but he's never been one for subtlety. His dance partner isn't complaining, so Kyle presses his palms against bare skin and pulls the guy back against him. "So, which one are we doing this for?"

The guy laughs and Kyle can feel the clench of his stomach beneath his hands. "The one looking at us."

It's Kyle's turn to laugh. "Do you really think it's only one?"

There's a whole line of people at the bar, drinks in hand, openly staring. Kyle sweeps his gaze over them, dismissing the ones who're ogling. He dips his thumb into the guy's waistband and tugs it down an inch. It flashes the jut of his hipbone, and Kyle grins as the man at the far end of the bar narrows his eyes.

"Bingo," Kyle says.

He ducks his head to press his face against his dance partner's neck. He's sweaty but still smells faintly of cologne. Will it match his partner's? Maybe the guy at the bar put cologne on before coaxing Kyle's dance partner into a lingering kiss until some of the scent transferred. Maybe it was his cologne, but he dotted it behind his partner's ears as a sign he has someone he's coming home to.

Kyle grins against skin and the man in his arms shudders. They aren't kissing, and Kyle isn't biting, but he knows what they look like. They could be doing anything here on the dance floor. The look in his eye as he meets the gaze of the man at the bar dares him to come and see.

He laughs as the guy pushes off the bar counter. "We're about to have company."

Bar Guy crosses the small strip of space between the bar and the dance floor. He looks them both over. "Having fun?"

"Not as much as he's about to be having." Kyle nudges his dance partner toward Bar Guy.

The guy Kyle had been dancing with goes easily into his partner's arms, but he turns so he's facing Kyle. "Do you want to dance a few more with us?"

It's tempting, but they're clearly together, and Kyle's too selfish to dance with people whose full attention isn't on him. He learned early on in his experimentation threesomes are only fun if he's the center of attention.

"I'm good. I have someone waiting for me at home."

Both men look surprised.

"He doesn't like to watch, but he doesn't mind me talking about it." Kyle blows them a kiss and disappears into the crowd again.

This time, he doesn't look for someone else to dance with. He heads straight for the coat check. Tonight's been fun, but he knows someone even better is waiting.

Kyle and Aidan have been together for almost half a year now. From the moment Kyle spotted him at his favorite club, he was on a mission to make Aidan notice him. He succeeded and after a trial period to see how their interests lined up, they agreed to three months together. Now they're two months into a six-month extension, their initial attraction only growing with each scene they share together.

He hopes the next time they sit down to talk about the direction of their relationship they'll extend things without an end date to hover over them.

This is his first time doing extended monogamy. He's never found a partner who matched up with him so well that he doesn't want anyone else but Aidan's different. Even where they're not exact fits—Kyle's more of an exhibitionist than Aidan's comfortable with—they find ways to make it work.

Like tonight.

Kyle hit the club and let over a dozen different men put their hands on him. He let them touch him and whisper shit in his ear while they ground up on him. He has sweat drying against his back and a mixture of colognes clinging to his clothes, the imprint of other men all over him. But Aidan's the one he's coming home to.

That's what does it for him. Well, he's vain enough that he enjoys showing off and being admired, but the true appeal of a night like this is receiving half a dozen offers and knowing there's someone better for him. It's what he wants to show Aidan too. He wants to tell him about all the men he could've gone home with, but instead, he chose Aidan. He'll choose him every time as long as Aidan is an option.

It's probably something he should say with words instead of a night of dancing then sex, but he's never had much patience with words. *Show, don't tell*, his English teachers always told him.

This probably isn't what they had in mind.

When he pulls into Aidan's driveway, he takes a deep breath before he turns off the ignition. This is the moment the whole night has led up to and now he's here, he wants to draw it out a little longer.

He walks quietly to the front door because Aidan lives in a duplex, and he doesn't want to disturb the couple who live in the other half of the house. He eases the door open and pauses because Aidan's sitting an armchair with a view of the front door. The reading light is on, and it makes it feel as if he's been waiting up for Kyle. He has, but between the single light and Kyle's soft tread, it's like he's been caught trying to sneak into the house.

He closes the door behind him.

Aidan slips a bookmark into his novel and closes it. "Did you have fun?"

Kyle grins, unable to help it. "Yeah."

"You're not too tired for more?" It's Aidan's turn to smile because he already knows what the answer will be.

"Definitely not." He sounds eager and doesn't care. He's not ashamed of wanting Aidan or having Aidan know it. Part of him wishes he'd stayed out later, until three a.m., so he could prove that even if he came home exhausted he'd want Aidan to lay him out and fuck him.

"I want you to wash up to your elbows, soap and warm water, then meet me in the guest bedroom."

It's a weird request, but Kyle obeys. He's disappointed in the lack of welcome-home kiss. He hopes kissing isn't completely off the table for tonight. He licks his lips, salty from sweat with a lingering sweetness from his lemonade. Should he brush his teeth or swish around some mouthwash?

Aidan didn't tell him to. He'd been very specific in what he wanted and Kyle wants to please.

He drapes his jacket over the bathroom door and runs the water until it's warm. He carefully washes his hands and wrists then his forearms until they're clean. He pats them dry and it makes him uncomfortably aware of how dirty the rest of him is.

Aidan's already in the bedroom when Kyle gets there. He pulls the comforter back from the bed and drapes it on the floor. The top sheet follows. Kyle's cuffs rest on the pillow closest to the door, and he takes a step toward them without realizing it right away.

They're brown leather and still fairly new. They were a gift from Aidan near the end of their three-month extension. Before, they used a black pair Kyle's had for years, but these are better. They're only for the two of them. No one else has seen Kyle in them, no one else has lovingly buckled them around Kyle's wrist. There are no memories pressed into their padding except the ones Kyle and Aidan have put there together.

As Kyle stares at them, he realizes why Aidan insisted he wash his hands and arms. He doesn't want strangers' sweat touching them. He probably doesn't need to worry about feelings going both ways.

Done fussing with the bed, Aidan turns his attention to Kyle. His gaze takes in Kyle's jeans, stiff, and his shirt, translucent, then reaches his face. He picks up the first cuff and turns it over in his hands. "Do you want this?"

It's the first of their check-ins, Aidan making sure they're still on for the plans they made earlier this week. If Kyle says no then they'll shower, separately, and sleep, together. But Kyle won't say no.

"I do," Kyle says. "But first..." He steps into Aidan's space and kisses him.

He was denied his kiss when he walked in the front door, and if kissing isn't in tonight's plans, then he wants this one before they begin their scene. It's softer than the kisses Kyle usually initiates, but the insistent need from the club is gone. He kisses Aidan as he thinks about how he had him wash his wrists so they'd be clean when Aidan put his cuffs on. Their lips move against each other and Kyle's fingers twitch, wanting to hold Aidan's because he sat up waiting for Kyle to come home.

He planned this entire night because Kyle asked for it, and Kyle wants to show how much he's enjoyed it so far and that he's looking forward to the rest.

Kyle breaks the kiss before he wants to—he'd kiss Aidan forever if he had his way. "I'm ready now."

He holds his wrist out and Aidan carefully buckles the leather around it. He slips a finger underneath to check it isn't too tight even though they've done this a dozen times by now. Would he do the same if Kyle wore his collar? The press of Aidan's finger against the smooth skin of Kyle's wrist is almost too much. He's not sure he'd be able to handle Aidan checking the fit of his collar.

Aidan does the second cuff as Kyle stares at him, eyes wide and breath already short.

Once warm leather is securely fastened around each of his wrists, Aidan takes a step back to look him over again. This look is different than the first one. It's assessing and Kyle stands taller. It makes him wish he didn't have any clothes on. Or that he had more.

His fingers tangle in the hem of his shirt. It seemed like the right choice when he picked it out, loose and light enough that it wouldn't be unbearable to dance in. But now he's out of the dark lighting of the dance club, he's aware of how flimsy it is.

Aidan steps up to Kyle, close enough that Kyle wants to take a step back so he can keep looking at Aidan's face but too far for them to be touching. He's caught in between two things, unsure of which he wants more. On a different day, in a different headspace, he'd be okay with it. He'd relax, knowing Aidan would pick the right one.

Kyle isn't there tonight, and he's not sure he wants to be.

"Touch me," he says. "Please."

Aidan's lips curl up in a smile. He steps close enough for their thighs to touch. He slides a hand down Kyle's back until it rests on Kyle's ass. He curls his other hand around Kyle's neck. "Like this?"

Kyle nods. Then shakes his head. It's a good start, but he wants more. He spent all night thinking about what Aidan would do to him when he came home and he's home now.

Aidan slides his hand into Kyle's back pocket. "I could put some music on. You weren't out very late. We can pick up where you left off."

Kyle's trembling, obvious enough that Aidan must notice, but he doesn't do anything. He stands there, watching, waiting, so Kyle moves closer. He pushes until he can fit them together, one of Aidan's thighs pressed between Kyle's.

It still isn't enough. Maybe Aidan *should* put on some music. But that won't be enough either. If he wanted to dance, he would've stayed at the club. He came home for Aidan and all the other ways they can fit themselves together.

If Kyle wants to move things along, and he does, then he'll have to nudge Aidan in the right direction.

"Do you know how many people touched me like this tonight?" Kyle asks.

Aidan squeezes the back of Kyle's neck, a warning, but Kyle doesn't know which one of them it's for. He knows Aidan doesn't like being overly possessive. He doesn't like the way it makes him feel or the things it makes him want to say or do.

But that wasn't what tonight was about.

"None of them were who I wanted," Kyle says, his words spoken against Aidan's cheek. He fidgets with Aidan's shirt. He wants to pull it off, but he'd have to step away to pull it over his head and he isn't willing to do that yet. "And none of them touched me the way I'm going to let you touch me tonight."

Aidan groans and pulls him in for a bruising kiss. He kisses like he's trying to leave an imprint of his mouth against Kyle's. Kyle moans into the kiss. He abandons his plans for Aidan's shirt and tugs at his pants instead.

Aidan catches Kyle's wrist in a firm hold. He could easily break his grip, but Aidan's fingers press against skin and leather, a reminder that he's agreed to play by Aidan's rules. If Aidan wants him to be still, then he'll be still.

"Good," Aidan says, the word breathed heavy between them.

Aidan walks them back toward the bed and Kyle drops down onto it. Aidan has to lean down to kiss him like this, and he breaks the kiss after only a few seconds. Kyle starts to sit up, chasing Aidan's mouth.

"Clothes off," Aidan says.

It's an order and a promise. As soon as Kyle pulls his shirt over his head, Aidan does the same. Kyle scrambles to tug his socks off then he's faced with the challenge of his pants. They're not his tightest pair, but they've suctioned to his legs.

He shoves them to his thighs before he looks up at Aidan, defeated.

Aidan laughs and pulls on the ends as Kyle shoves them from the top. Between the two of them, his jeans end up in a pile on the floor. After that, his briefs are easy to take off. It feels good to be naked. It's even better when Aidan's naked in front of him too.

It's not something he does all the time. When they first started out, Kyle thought it was a *thing*. Apparently it wasn't but the more desperate he grew to see Aidan, the more pleasure Aidan took in denying him.

Tonight, though, they're both naked, and Kyle's attention is on Aidan's cock. It's half-hard, and Aidan's close enough that he could easily reach out and touch it. He keeps his hands at his sides but asks, "Can I suck you?"

"No," Aidan answers and smiles at Kyle's groan.

"I'd make it good."

They've been together long enough that Kyle knows what Aidan likes. He knows how to get him off quickly, how to tease him, and how to give a blowjob that leaves them both shaking by the end of it.

"I want your mouth free," Aidan says. He runs his hands through Kyle's hair and tips his head back for another kiss.

When they break their kiss, Aidan makes a half-hearted effort to put Kyle's hair back into some kind of order. Then he shrugs. "Get the lube," he says.

Kyle crawls across the bed so he can reach the far nightstand. He grabs the bottle and then holds up a condom, questioning.

Aidan shakes his head as he sits against the headboard, his legs stretched out in front of him. Kyle joins him, straddling his thighs.

"What do you want my mouth free for?" he asks, dropping the bottle on the bed next to them. "Are you ready to hear about my night?"

Aidan runs his hands up the backs of Kyle's thighs, touching as much skin as he can before he traces the same path back down. Kyle spreads his legs, encouraging Aidan to touch more, and he grins when Aidan smacks his thigh.

The sting fades too quickly. Is it too late to add a quick spanking to the night's agenda? He's been touched by dozens of people tonight, but none of them left any kind of lingering mark. He wants to wake up tomorrow with the evidence of Aidan's touch. He wants to look in the mirror and know who he belongs to.

He curls his fingers around Aidan's shoulders. "Do you want me to start at the beginning or do you want least interesting to most interesting?"

Aidan slides his hands up Kyle's thighs again, higher and higher, but then they skip his ass to trail up his back instead.

"I picked the perfect pair of jeans," Kyle says. "They were tight enough to show off my body but not so tight that a guy couldn't slip his hand into my back pocket."

Aidan laughs as he cups Kyle's ass. "Is this what you want?" He squeezes, nails biting into Kyle's skin. Kyle wants to move into the touch as much as he wants to move away from it.

"More," he says.

Aidan drops his hands lower again. His nails drag too lightly, and Kyle squirms, wanting it harder.

"Were you this demanding with your dance partners?"

Kyle isn't sure why he thought tonight would end with Aidan tossing him on the bed and fucking the thought of anyone else out of his head. Aidan has an uncanny ability to know exactly what Kyle wants but not give it to him. He's a tease, and Kyle would hate it more if he didn't love the way it twists him up, winding him tighter and tighter until Aidan finally does something.

"I didn't have to be," Kyle answers. "They gave me what I wanted. Well, some of it."

Aidan raises his eyebrows.

"I knew the best part of my night would happen when I came home." Kyle leans in to kiss Aidan because touching his shoulders isn't enough. He kisses him hard, trying to convey how glad he is to be here. He doesn't mind starting his night somewhere else, but he wants to end it here. Always.

It's a lot to try to get across with a kiss, but Kyle gives it his best shot.

When they finally break their kiss, Kyle tucks his face against Aidan's neck.

"They didn't kiss you," Aidan says. It isn't a question, but Kyle nods anyway. Aidan moves one of his hands then Kyle hears the click of the lube. "They didn't do this either." Aidan presses a finger against Kyle's hole, not pushing in, just resting there.

"They didn't, but some of them wanted to."

"I can't blame them for that." Aidan works Kyle open, one finger then more lube as he adds a second. Kyle tries to hold himself still, but he's been waiting for too long.

He rises up higher on his knees so he can sink down on Aidan's fingers. He tips his head back as he's filled.

"Stop it," Aidan says.

"I want it," Kyle whines but he stops moving. It's Aidan's show now which means he has to let him set the pace even if Aidan's preferred way of doing things is maddeningly slow. "I've thought about it all night."

"All night?"

"Yes." Kyle meets Aidan's gaze head on so the man can see his desperation and his honesty. "Every time someone pulled me back against them and ground their dick against my ass, I thought about how it was only a few more dances before I'd be able to come home and get it for real. This entire night was a tease. Please, give me a third finger. I want you to fuck me."

Aidan stubbornly continues to scissor him with two fingers. He doesn't even stretch Kyle as much as he could. If Kyle could only move, then he'd be able to get something out of this. Instead, he curls his fingers until he clings to Aidan's shoulder, taking the one thing he's been allowed.

"Be patient," Aidan says.

He's been nothing but patient all night. Well, he's *waited*. He wouldn't say he's done it patiently, but he's done it long enough. He's home, he's naked, he's in Aidan's bed and these things should all add up to what he wants, but he's not quite there.

"I was invited home by a couple," Kyle says. He's not allowed to move, he's not allowed to beg for what he wants, but Aidan hasn't told him he can't talk. "My last partner of the night sought me out. He probably watched me for a few songs and realized he liked what he was seeing."

Kyle tips his head back and groans as Aidan scrapes his teeth down the exposed line of his neck. He won't leave any marks there, but he can still shiver at the possibility of them. Maybe next time he goes dancing, he can wear Aidan's marks up and down his neck. Or his cuffs, a sign to everyone there that he's taken and there's no offer they can make him that's better than the one waiting for him at home.

"I didn't have the man's full attention," Kyle says, continuing his story. "He kept looking over at the bar. He was putting on a show and using me to help him."

"I bet you helped him."

"I figured out what he was doing and told him we could make it look good." Kyle leans back enough for Aidan to see the spark in his eye and the smirk tugging at his lips. "It didn't take long for his partner to come join us."

"I'm sure it didn't." Aidan moves his mouth lower to Kyle's collarbone. He sets his teeth against the dip of it and leaves a mark that Kyle's clothes will cover later.

Kyle clenches down around Aidan's fingers and can't help his small whine. He doesn't understand how he can feel so empty when he's *full*. He rolls his hips down, chasing Aidan's fingers, but it isn't enough. Aidan pulls out of him, and tears spring into Kyle's eyes.

"Do you want me to beg?" Kyle asks. He's tried asking for what he wants, tried telling Aidan about the people who were willing to give it to him. He doesn't know what else he can do.

"Not tonight." Aidan pets Kyle's thigh, an apology or maybe a reassurance. "I want you to ride me."

Finally.

They're so close that when Aidan slicks his cock up, his knuckles brush the underside of Kyle's. Kyle wants to press into the contact, but Aidan's promised to give him what he wants tonight. It means trusting and waiting even if a minute seems too long.

Once Aidan's ready, he holds his cock steady and says, "Slowly now."

Kyle grits his teeth and forces himself to take Aidan's cock as slowly as he can. His legs tremble as he lowers himself down. He curls his hands in and out of fists because part of him needs to move. It isn't enough, or maybe it's too much as his body makes space for Aidan inside him.

This slowly, he feels every inch. He has to pause and turn his face into Aidan's neck when he's only half-seated. His thighs quake with the effort to hold still, but he needs a moment to breathe. His arms are wrapped around Aidan's neck and his face is pressed against sweaty skin and it feels like a dozen different dances he had tonight.

But when he wakes up in the morning, he won't think about those dances and the men who offered to buy him drinks or take him home.

He'll think about *Aidan.*

He kisses Aidan, desperation in the press of his lips and bite of his teeth. If he doesn't kiss him, then he'll talk, and embarrassing things will spill out of his mouth. The kiss is rough and hurried, a counterpoint to how slowly he takes Aidan's cock again. He wants to drop down and feel the burn of too much too fast before it melts into just right. He wants the air punched out of his lungs and the words expelled from his mouth until he's filled with need and a desire for more.

It isn't what Aidan wants, though, and above all, Kyle wants to be good for the other man.

His pace is glacial even as his hands slide into Aidan's hair and tip his head back so their kiss grows sharper. Kyle takes here the way he can't there, losing himself in Aidan's mouth. He clutches Aidan's shoulders and curls his fingers around his hair.

When he's finally seated on Aidan's cock, Aidan tugs on Kyle's hair until their kiss is broken and they're looking at each other. Dizzy with how Aidan's on him and *in* him, all around him and yet still not close enough, it takes Kyle a moment to focus.

Aidan cards a hand through Kyle's hair, and his eyes flutter as if he wants to close them. A sharp pull has Kyle's eyes wide open and his attention on his Dom.

"Fuck yourself on my cock and make me come," Aidan says. His lips curl into a half-smile. "Unless you're too tired."

Kyle shakes his head and eagerly proves it. He rises up on his knees and then sinks back down. He's sore from dancing, and he knows he'll wake up even sorer tomorrow, but he won't pass up an opportunity to make Aidan come. Kyle's the one who spent the past few hours having fun while Aidan sat at home waiting for him. He wants to make sure Aidan's night is as good as his has been.

This is why he came home, he thinks, his quads flexing as he fucks down on Aidan's cock. Anyone in the club could've made him feel good, but Aidan's the one Kyle wants and he wasn't there. He was at home, waiting for Kyle to come back to him and prove that even with an entire dance floor full of temptation, Kyle knows exactly who he wants.

"You," Kyle murmurs as he rides Aidan's cock.

"You," he says between kisses to Aidan's cheeks, his jaw, his lips.

"You," he repeats, over and over, as he chases Aidan's orgasm, his own a distant thought in his head.

When Aidan comes, he curls his fingers around Kyle's hips, and his short nails dig into Kyle's skin, small pinpricks of pain that keep Kyle here and present.

He has leather cuffs on his wrists which say he belongs to Aidan, but with every word Kyle utters, with every kiss he presses against Aidan's skin, he makes the same claim. Aidan is *his*. There's no bed he'd rather be in and no one else he'd rather share it with.

Aidan tips them over so Kyle's on his back on the bed. Aidan's over him now, covering him with his body. It's almost perfect and Kyle tips his face up for a kiss. Aidan doesn't kiss him. Then he pulls out and that's...that's even less than perfect.

Kyle whines, unhappy to be empty. He had been full and covered, blanketed and obviously cared for and now Aidan's moving away from him. It's the exact opposite of what he wants.

Aidan's smile is fond as he runs his fingers over the red marks on Kyle's hip. With his other hand, he slides two fingers back into Kyle. "Better?"

"Bite me?" Kyle asks. Later tonight when Aidan's asleep, he wants to feel the throb of Aidan's marks, a reminder of tonight. Tomorrow morning, he wants to wake up to see a map of this spread across his skin. He can't keep Aidan inside him forever. He can't even keep Aidan at his side for that long. But Aidan can leave behind reminders and promises to carry Kyle through until the next time they're together.

Even though he asked to be bitten, Kyle surges up for a kiss. He drags their mouths together and kisses Aidan until Aidan slides a third finger into him. Kyle parts his lips and moans. His rolls his hips down, searching for more. His cock bobs between their bodies, hard and leaking.

Aidan kisses the corner of Kyle's mouth and then moves down. His lips are gentle against the curve of his jaw then even gentler against his neck. Kyle shudders and clenches down around Aidan's fingers and it's almost enough. He draws in a ragged breath as Aidan chuckles, breath ghosting over Kyle's overheated skin.

He moves down Kyle's body, everything too light, too soft, until he bites just above Kyle's belly button.

"More," Kyle asks. "Please."

Aidan lays stinging bites against Kyle's skin. He leaves behind red spots which will turn darker overnight. He spreads his fingers inside Kyle's body until all Kyle can feel is Aidan—his teeth and his fingers and the heat of his body as he leans over Kyle's.

It takes a well-timed twist of Aidan's fingers and the tight grip of his hand for Kyle to come. Aidan looks at his hand, splattered with come, and wipes it on Kyle's chest. He eases his fingers out of Kyle's body and watches Kyle's face as he does it as though looking for any twitch or sign of discomfort.

If Kyle didn't feel every last bit of his strength had been sapped from him then he'd frown. Or maybe not. Because the second-best part of the night is here now. Aidan will wipe them both down and then climb into bed with him. Kyle can cuddle as close as he wants, drawing as much warmth and security from Aidan as he'd like.

"Thank you," Kyle murmurs, eyes already slipping closed.

"Thank *you*." Aidan brushes his lips over Kyle's and lightly slaps at his cheek. "You aren't allowed to sleep yet."

"Sounds fake." With every breath he takes, Kyle sinks deeper into the mattress. As soon as he closes his eyes, he'll fall asleep, and he can't think of a single reason why he wouldn't want that.

"Shower first," Aidan coaxes. "Someone came home smelling like smoke and cheap beer." He nuzzles Kyle's neck before Kyle can work out whether he's being chastised. "A quick shower, a change of sheets, and we can sleep."

Showering means he has to take his cuffs off, and Kyle stares at his bare wrists, too white without the strip of brown leather cradling them. A fissure of wrong worms its way into his pleasant haze but before it can spread too far, Aidan circles his fingers around one of Kyle's wrists.

"I'm here," Aidan promises, drawing Kyle closer. "I'll be here the whole time. You don't want to fall asleep covered in come."

He doesn't because then he has to wake up that way, and that's never fun. He allows himself to be led into the shower, and he rinses off the sweat and the come and the lube. Aidan's boring body wash erases any hint of the bar.

When they step out of the shower, Kyle's clean from head to foot. The only things left over from tonight are the marks scattered across his body and the pleasant soreness in his legs. He'll wake up with both of those in the morning too, to look at and feel and remind him of all the good things that happened tonight.

Chapter Two

KYLE WAKES UP to Aidan tracing shapes on his stomach. The touch is too light to be what woke him up. He smiles because he wasn't the first awake and Aidan chose to linger in bed with him. He'd fallen asleep quickly last night, denying him important cuddling time. He intends to make up for it this morning.

"I know you're awake," Aidan says. His fingers tap-tap over Kyle's heart. "Your breathing changed. Also, you're smiling."

He is. He's full out beaming as he opens his eyes and looks up at Aidan. "Hey."

Aidan laughs but says, "Hey," back. The laughter fades from his eyes. "How are you feeling?"

"Hungry. Breakfast?"

"Are you asking if I'm hungry or if I have food in the house which can be eaten at this time of day?"

Kyle's still grinning as he slides out of bed. It's easy to leave the warm cocoon of the blankets and Aidan's touch because he knows Aidan will follow him. They'll make breakfast together; well, Kyle will make breakfast while Aidan watches then they'll eat together.

"You've gotten better at keeping your place stocked," Kyle says.

Aidan used to live on microwaveable meals and things that only required a pot of boiling water and a box with simple instructions. He still eats those things when

Kyle isn't around, but if Kyle's here, then he cooks for the two of them and tries to leave enough leftovers in the fridge to tide Aidan over until the next time he stops by.

"I'll start the coffee," Aidan says.

"I'll be there in a minute."

Kyle stops in the bathroom to take a piss and brush his teeth. His cuffs are on the counter where they left them before the shower last night. He trails a finger over them before spitting his toothpaste into the sink. He wants them back on.

He knows the scene is over, that was last night, and they've moved into a quiet morning designed to settle both of them. But he wants the steady pressure of the leather wrapped around his wrists, a promise that he's held and cared for. That's too close to a collar, and Kyle snatches his hand back.

Cuffs signal to him whether he's in a scene or not. Cuffs on means game on. Cuffs off means it's over. A collar is something different. Wearing one would mean he belongs to his Dom whether they're in a scene or not. It's something he's always wanted, the reassurance it would bring, but he's never found the right person.

Maybe at the end of this six-month extension, he and Aidan will be in a place where they can talk about collars. Aidan was the one to give Kyle his new cuffs; this time Kyle will be able to offer him something. He already has the collar he wants, hidden in a box in his closet. He keeps it on the top shelf, away from his box of toys so he won't see it when he brings someone home to scene with.

It's brown leather, thick and sturdy. Without even realizing it, Aidan bought cuffs that would match it. He wants Aidan to be the first person to buckle the collar around his neck. He touches his fingers to his neck and closes his eyes as he imagines how gentle Aidan's hands would be.

He snaps his eyes open before his fantasy can go too far. He and Aidan are compatible in a lot of ways, but he shouldn't push for too much. He doesn't want to ruin the good thing they have.

But it could be better...

He splashes his face with water.

This is his first time in a long-term monogamous partnership and he's jumping the gun. Renee, one of his partners before Aidan, would scene with him a couple times a month and they'd sometimes do breakfast in the morning before going their separate ways. They never had a formal relationship like he does with Aidan and they were never monogamous. The closest he's had to that is the fledgling Doms he worked with. Monogamy and schedules were both important to the mentoring process.

This is his first time being exclusive because of feelings.

It's different and leaves him off-balance whenever he's least expecting it.

He pulls on a pair of plaid pajama pants before heading into the kitchen. Aidan's staring at the coffee machine as it percolates as if somehow he can make it brew faster. Kyle drops a kiss against Aidan's cheek before opening the fridge.

There are eggs and he even has milk that isn't expired. Neither of these was guaranteed before Kyle began spending time here. He smiles as he sees more of his influence; a fresh pepper, half a cucumber, and an onion wrapped in plastic. He pulls out the pepper and the onion and a block of cheese. The milk and eggs are next.

"Pancakes?" Kyle asks, spotting the yellow Bisquick box. Pancakes, eggs, and sausage if Aidan has it in his freezer.

"Sounds good."

Aidan hands a cup of coffee to Kyle and keeps the second for himself. His eyes dip down as Kyle accepts the offered mug. A frown wrinkles his forehead, and Kyle can't help but look down too, wondering what's wrong. Kyle's shirtless and his pajama pants are slung low, but that should make Aidan smile.

Aidan's handiwork—mouthwork?—is on full display. Kyle's torso is covered in little bites and marks. There are fingerprint bruises at his hips. Kyle got caught up staring at them in the bedroom earlier, and he made sure they were visible when he wandered in. He likes looking down and seeing the reminder of last night mapped out on his skin.

But Aidan's gaze skitters away, never landing in one place for long. It isn't the usual reaction Kyle gets when he's shirtless. He's used to lingering, heated stares,

Kyle sets the Bisquik next to the mixing bowl and then turns away from breakfast. "What's wrong?"

"Nothing."

It's a bullshit answer, and Kyle knows his expression says so.

Aidan huffs a little. He tries to look away, but his gaze is pulled back to Kyle's hip where a particularly dark bruise stands out. "Sometimes I feel guilty."

Progress, even if Kyle doesn't understand. He leaves his coffee and steps into Aidan's space, hoping to offer some comfort. Even if Aidan feels guilty, Kyle doesn't. He trusts him and wants to be near him, as close as Aidan will allow.

"Guilty about what?"

Aidan's fingers brush the marks on Kyle's hips; the bruises from where Aidan's fingers pressed hard into his skin and the red marks left behind by his teeth. He can't help his smile, thinking about how Aidan had held him as he fucked him and the sharp sting of his teeth when Kyle asked for it.

Kyle only has good feelings associated with the marks and the memory of last night. He wants Aidan to feel the same way.

"I begged you for these," Kyle says. He covers Aidan's hands so that Aidan's palms press flat against his skin. "I wanted them then and I still want them now."

"You don't know what I was thinking when I left them."

Aidan frees a hand so he can brush his knuckles across Kyle's neck. Kyle tips his head back, baring his throat.

"I wanted to leave a mark here," Aidan continues. "I wanted to make sure that when you walk out my front door, everyone will know you belong to me."

Kyle takes a slow, measured breath, but he can't control the way his pulse jumps at Aidan's words. There's no way Aidan misses it with his fingers right there. He wouldn't mind if Aidan marked him like that. Well, not exactly like that, because a giant hickey on his neck isn't professional. But the sentiment behind it? He *wants* Aidan to claim him.

Maybe, next time he goes out, it will be to Enchanting Encounters, and he'll wear an outfit showing Aidan's claim. He'll have a drink and drift through the bar, chatting with his friends and the regulars. He'll invite people to look at him and know that besides seeing a fit body, they'll see he's off limits.

Or, Aidan will take him to the dance club and keep him close, an arm around his waist or a hand on the back of his neck. They'll dance for hours and no one will matter but the two of them. No one will even dare approach, because Kyle won't be there for them. Not that time.

When he returns to the present, Aidan's frowning again, the wrinkle wedged even deeper into his forehead. Kyle aches to smooth it away.

"I wanted you to mark me," Kyle reminds him. "I spent the night out, and I came home for *you*. You didn't do anything I didn't like. Or anything I didn't ask for."

"I'm the one who's supposed to have a level head," Aidan says. "I find it difficult around you."

"Bullshit." Kyle's sympathy evaporates in a flash. "We're both responsible for keeping things safe and fun for both of us. You're worried about feeling possessive? We can talk through it and plan our scenes accordingly but don't act as if I'm too deep in my headspace or too passive to put a stop to something I don't like."

Aidan opens his mouth—to apologize? Sway Kyle to his point? Kyle has an idea of where this is coming from. Aidan's last relationship didn't end well. His sub was new to the scene and too focused on Aidan to keep himself in his thoughts. It didn't end well and now Aidan doubts himself.

Kyle understands that, and he has his own triggers he's careful to work around in scenes. They can work around Aidan's but not if Aidan's trying to pass it off as being for Kyle's own good.

"I like it when you pin me to the bed as if you think I'll get away if you don't hold me down," Kyle says, capturing Aidan's full attention. "I like it when you growl against my neck and bite promises into my skin. I like pushing you to the edge of your control just like you push me to the edge of mine."

Aidan's guilt is written clear across his face. Kyle catches his chin between his fingers, gentle, and keeps Aidan's focus on him.

"I wouldn't do any of that if I didn't trust you. There are things I like in a scene and things I fantasize about that I'd never want in reality. The thoughts in your head don't scare me, because thought doesn't always mean action. You can want things that scare you, you can want things that scare me, but I won't be scared of you because I know you won't act on them."

"That's a lot of faith to have in me."

"You've never given me a reason to doubt you," Kyle says. He allows his hand to drop away. It feels wrong not to be touching Aidan, but the man probably wants some space right now. "Would you like me to put a shirt on? I don't want to make you uncomfortable."

"I like them," Aidan confesses, quiet. He reaches out as if he wants to touch before he pulls his hand back. "Sometimes I feel like I shouldn't."

Kyle looks down at his bare chest. "I wanted them and you gave them to me. There's nothing wrong with that. I want to show them off now because they remind me of last night. I'll cover them with a shirt later because they aren't for Ritchie or Jenny or Charlotte. They're about you and me and last night. But that's what they mean to me. If it's different for you, then I'll put my shirt on now."

Aidan shakes his head. "It sounds better when you say it than when I think about it in my head."

"That's because you're thinking the worst right now." Kyle's head gets twisted like that sometimes. He leans in to press a chaste kiss to Aidan's lips. "How about this;

we'll eat breakfast then we go back to bed. You can kiss every mark you gave me, and I'll tell you how much I wanted them. Then I'll tell you how they'll remind me of you during the week when you're teaching your classes and I'm working, and we aren't together."

"That sounds like a plan."

Kyle smiles and pushes a little. "The *best* plan."

"Yeah, yeah," Aidan says, but he smiles. "Will you show me how to make pancakes?"

"I show you every week. This is just an excuse for you to crowd me while I'm cooking."

Aidan's smile grows as he presses himself against Kyle's back, arms wrapped loosely around Kyle's waist. "Do you feel crowded?"

Kyle leans back into Aidan's hold. "Nah." He twists, looking for a kiss.

Aidan gives it to him, but the angle is awkward like this. When Kyle tries to twist to face him, Aidan holds his hips steady.

"Breakfast first," Aidan says.

Kyle groans.

"It's your plan," Aidan reminds him, sounding too smug. "I believe someone said something about the best plan."

Kyle groans again but cracks an egg into the mixing bowl.

KYLE HAS COMPANY waiting for him in his apartment. Jenny's sprawled across his couch, munching on Cheetos. Her hair is black right now, the tips dyed cotton candy pink. It's short enough that it doesn't stay tucked neatly behind her ears.

She shakes it out of her face only to scowl when the strands fall back in front of her eyes. "Ugh. Remind me never to cut my hair short again."

Jenny is Kyle's closest friend. They met in middle school, becoming inseparable after a month of riding the late bus together. Jenny would stay after school twice a week, once for art club and once for photography club. Kyle was in art club too, but when she was in photography club, he was in cooking club.

Middle school wasn't an easy time for a boy to be interested in cooking, but instead of laughing at him, Jenny asked how come he didn't bring anything to share with her if they were friends. He'd said something like, "We're friends?" and she'd laughed and told him of course they were.

The next week, instead of eating both of his muffins, he brought one for her.

Now, they live down the hall from each other and have keys to each other's apartments which leads to moments like this.

"I didn't know I had Cheetos," he says.

"You don't. I brought these with me."

That makes more sense. "Where's Charlotte?" It's Sunday night which means where one of them is, the other shouldn't be far behind.

Jenny's eyebrows pull together in a frown. Kyle always expects the barbells she has pieced through them to clink, but she can't quite bring her eyebrows close enough together.

"Family dinner," Jenny answers.

That explains why Jenny's on his couch, eating Cheetos and watching *Buffy the Vampire Slayer*. Charlotte's family is conservative and they nudged their daughter toward being a librarian hoping it would be the modern-day equivalent of locking her in a tower. Well, that's what Kyle assumes. He's never met Charlotte's family.

Jenny's only met them once.

They hate Jenny's tattoos and they hate her piercings and they hate that she's dating their daughter and they really don't like that she's a freelance photographer. Apparently they think it's code for porn.

After that first meeting, Jenny was slotted into the "going to ruin our daughter" category, and she hasn't found her way out of it yet. It means no invites to family dinner which means Kyle occasionally ends up with a mopey house guest.

He wishes Charlotte's family would direct their dislike at him and let Jenny and Charlotte be happy. After all, it is Kyle who introduced them. He was contacted by the local library to do some promotional work for them. He's a graphic designer and they wanted flyers done for an upcoming fundraiser.

He did most of his work in the library itself because it was quiet and had Wi-Fi, his two requirements for a long-term working space. Of course, he missed an important third requirement.

Food.

Turns out, librarians get scowly when people eat in their building.

"There's no food in the library," he was told after being caught with a bag of carrots.

The librarian scolding him fit his stereotype—a homemade sweater with Clifford on it, glasses dangling from a chain around her neck, and a pair of shoes that looked like they belonged in a museum. The only thing missing was she wasn't pushing retirement age. She was almost half a decade too young for that.

When she realized he was the guy working on their flyers, she invited him to the staff room where he was allowed to eat while he worked.

He finished the job and then, figuring it couldn't hurt to support the library, he actually showed up to the fundraiser, some date night with a book thing. He brought Jenny with him and she met Charlotte and—well, the rest is history.

He lifts Jenny's feet so he can sit on the couch with her. "If you eat the whole bag then you won't have room for what Charlotte brings home."

Because Charlotte always brings dessert home: cake, some kind of berry crumble, a chocolate chip cookie that she'll heat up so the chocolate chips are melted again. Jenny thinks it's some kind of poor consolation prize. Kyle thinks it's Charlotte's way of trying to include her.

"Whatever," Jenny says. She takes a defiant handful of the orange snack and chews as obnoxiously as she can.

She does put the bag down after that, though, and they watch Buffy kick ass for a couple of minutes.

"How was your weekend?" Jenny asks.

"Good." On a different night, he might give her more details, but he doesn't want to come across as gloating.

"We missed you last night. We went to the club."

Enchanting Encounters is the kink club Kyle frequents. It's where he's met most of his scene partners over the years, including Aidan. He's friends with the owner, Wanda, and he does some graphic design work for her as well as some more hands-on work. He does demos and live shows and works with Doms new to the scene.

He hasn't done much of the latter since he and Aidan began their thing, but Kyle hopes that will change. He loves the look on a Dom's face when they realize something works for them. He still remembers his first real spanking. He'd played around with people, had a few adventurous hookups, but the first time someone put him over their lap, a strong hand on the back of his neck and an even stronger one laying on the blows, his brain stuttered to a halt before becoming a litany of *yes yes yes* that he hasn't looked back from.

He still loves scening, but the thrill of discovery is something which has faded as he spends more time in the lifestyle. Experiencing it vicariously is almost as good, and there's something satisfying about showing someone how good they can feel when everything clicks just right.

"I went dancing," Kyle tells her.

"Just you?"

"There were other people there."

She kicks him.

"Aidan stayed home," he says, answering the question she was really asking.

Jenny looks away from the TV. "Is something wrong?"

"It was a scene."

"Oh," she says, relieved. Then she wrinkles her nose. "I don't need any more details than that."

He laughs as he flicks the bottom of her foot. He's worked as a model for Jenny, letting her tie him up for demos at the club and photoshoots for her website, but that's as far as they take things. She has an artist's appreciation for the human form and no interest in him, and while he's bi, he's never been attracted to her.

And even if they were interested in each other, they're not well-matched. He had a bad experience with bondage once, a Dom who tied him up and left him. The only reason he can do it with Jenny is because he trusts her as much as he does. He knows she'll never leave him on his own. She's either right by his side as she creates her design or a couple of feet away with a camera, capturing it.

He can relax enough to look good for his audience, and he knows how to pose for a camera, but he can't lose himself the way he does in a scene.

Jenny kicks him again, lighter this time, claiming his attention. "Speaking of your man..." She pauses her episode. "The Bondage Expo is in May. I know it's still two months out, but I need to let them know if you'll be there with me."

The Expo is something Jenny attends every year. She gives lessons and demos and talks with other people who study and practice bondage. He goes with her every year to help with her demonstrations. He's never been in a relationship before when the Expo rolled around.

"I'll talk to Aidan get an answer for you this week."

"Do you think he might say no?"

"Maybe."

Jenny narrows her eyes, preparing herself for a fight.

"Settle down," Kyle says.

Relationships are about compromise and this is new. They'll talk about it out and either Kyle will go or he won't. He doesn't want to push Aidan into anything he's uncomfortable with.

"You haven't been around the club as much since you started up with him."

Kyle sighs. Looks like they're having this conversation whether he wants to or not. "I still go and yes, Aidan and I are going to talk about that too. I'd like to demo again, but it's something I want not something I need."

"Uh-huh. Just make sure that in all your compromising you're not always the one giving in."

He knows she's looking out for him so he doesn't snap at her. "I will. Now, are we watching *Buffy* or not?"

She unpauses the show and then flips around so that instead of her feet in his lap, she's tucked against his side.

"I just want you to be happy," she says.

"I know. I am. And I'm going to make sure I stay that way."

Chapter Three

AIDAN COMES OVER on Wednesday night, and he takes his shoes off by the door so he doesn't track slush through the apartment. It snowed last week, but a cold spell has kept it from melting completely. Kyle's welcome mat is streaked white with the salt they put down on the roads and sidewalks. He'll have to toss it and buy a new one as soon as winter is finally over.

Or he'll stick it in the closet to use next winter and have seasonal welcome mats.

"Lost in thought?" Aidan asks.

Kyle realizes that one, he hasn't said hello yet, and two, his oven is beeping at him.

"Floor mats," Kyle answers as he pulls the chicken out of the oven. He places the pan on a cooling rack and then turns off the oven.

When he turns around, Aidan's watching him, a half smile curling his lips. "Floor mats?"

"Not important. Where's my hello kiss?"

Aidan's full-out smiling now. He steps into Kyle's space and nudges him to the side so no one will accidentally touch the glass pan that just came out of the oven. Then he kisses Kyle, his lips cool and his cheeks even colder.

Kyle shivers but presses closer. He slips his hands up Aidan's shirt.

"Dinner," Aidan says after breaking the kiss.

He doesn't pull completely away so it's more of a token protest. Besides, "It needs a couple minutes to cool off anyway."

Aidan responds by brushing their cheeks against each other. He laughs when Kyle tries to squirm away and then ducks his head so his chilled skin presses against Kyle's neck instead.

"I'm feeling used," Kyle grumbles.

Aidan laughs and cups his hands around Kyle's neck.

Kyle tries to escape, but Aidan pins him against the counter, laughing again as Kyle scowls at him.

"Haven't you ever heard of gloves?"

"This is much more fun." Aidan kisses the frown right off Kyle's face. He pulls back soon enough that Kyle chases him until he's caught by Aidan's hands. Aidan's smile only grows. "I'm sorry, it sounded like you were unhappy."

Kyle knocks Aidan's loose grip away and pushes him up against the fridge, careful of the handles, and kisses him the way he's wanted to since Aidan first walked through the door. It's hot and messy, and a little hurried as if Kyle doesn't think they have enough time.

When Aidan's cold knuckles first brush against Kyle's stomach, he yelps and pulls back.

"Sorry," Aidan says and he actually does sound sorry this time.

"*Gloves.*"

"I forgot them," Aidan admits. "Well, I forgot my whole jacket. It was over the back of my desk chair, but I was caught up in my grading and when my alarm went off to remind to leave I was in a rush and..." He flashes a sheepish grin.

"I can't believe you went outside without a coat. Go run your hands under hot water or something. And put on a sweatshirt. Or two. I'll set dinner out."

"Double-layering sweatshirts?" Aidan's amusement lingers even as he heads down the hall for Kyle's room.

"Is that judgement I hear from someone who willingly wears elbow pads?"

"College professor chic!" Aidan calls. "It's a thing."

Alone in his kitchen, Kyle rolls his eyes. *College professor chic.* This is the man he chooses to spend time with; one who has to set alarms to pull him out of work and who wears tweed jackets with elbow pads. It would be embarrassing how far gone he is on Aidan if he didn't think Aidan felt the same way about him.

He sets the table and has dinner arranged on the small table tucked into the corner of his kitchen by the time Aidan emerges from the bedroom. He's in sweatpants a couple of inches too long and Kyle's favorite Henley. It's soft from repeated washes and beginning to wear through at the elbows.

He can't help his grin. "I might need to ask for your elbow patch guy soon."

Aidan shakes his head as he pulls down glasses for them. "Water?"

"Yeah, thanks."

Aidan pours them each a glass before taking his seat at the four-person table. Normally, Kyle eats standing at his island or sitting in front of his TV. The table is for when he's making an effort. Aidan would probably laugh if Kyle told him that, but he's worth making an effort for. Should he buy a tablecloth? It seems like a suitably adult thing to do. Should he have seasonal tablecloths the way he has seasonal welcome mats?

"How do you decorate a whole house?" Kyle asks.

"Technically, I think I only have to decorate half a house," Aidan answers. "But not well. Decorating feels too much like cluttering most of the time. Why?"

"I think I need to buy tablecloths. And a new welcome mat. Something springy."

Aidan's eyebrows pull together. "Springy? Are you buying a welcome mat or a trampoline?"

Kyle laughs as he cuts his chicken into bite-sized pieces. "Not that kind of springy. Like the season. Something with flowers. Or rain."

"You want a welcome mat with rainclouds on it? Are you sure you're a graphic designer? Your taste is terrible."

"*Tweed*," Kyle says. Then, offering a truce, "How was work today? Besides so busy you were almost late for dinner?"

"I wasn't almost late. And classes were good. One of my classes was a lecture, but another one of them was more discussion based. I'm always amazed that even though I teach some of the same classes every year, it's not boring. My students find ways of bringing unique insights and views to the material. Well, sometimes."

They talk about Aidan's classes, both today's and the next two days', and then they talk about Kyle's current projects.

Then Kyle brings up what he's been thinking about since he and Jenny talked on Sunday.

"So, there's a Bondage Expo coming up in May," he says as if there's a casual way to drop that kind of statement into a conversation.

Aidan looks confused at first before he nods and guesses, "Jenny?"

"This will be her sixth year being invited. I've gone with her every year to help demonstrate and because it's a fun trip. It's only three days, but with travel, we're usually gone longer."

"Early or late May?"

"Early."

"During finals for me. You'll be off having fun while I'm giving exams then grading them." He sounds wistful, a little jealous, but not angry.

Kyle doesn't want to ask for permission to attend, because the idea sits uncomfortably with him, but he still wants to make sure there won't be any problems if he does go. "You're cool with it?"

"It's with Jenny. It'll be like when you model for her, right? Artistic."

"It's not quite the same," Kyle explains. "There's a kink aspect to the weekend, but if you're saying it isn't sexual for me then yeah. It'll be like the demo we did at the club which...you didn't see."

Aidan's lips quirk up in a smile. "One of the demos that was part of Project: Notice Me?"

Kyle flushes all the way to the tips of his ears. "I shouldn't have told you about that. But yes. There'll be some touching, and there will definitely be people watching but nothing more than that. I only work with Jenny."

"It sounds like you'll have a good time."

Kyle hopes he doesn't look as relieved as he feels. He doesn't even need to give Aidan any of his carefully constructed reasons for why he wants to go and why it isn't a threat to their relationship. "We can plan some stuff to do while I'm there. Five days is a long time to go without seeing each other. I know you'll be busy with school stuff, but we both have computers and phones. Technology is pretty awesome."

"As long as it won't interfere with what you and Jenny are doing," Aidan says. There's the tiniest of frowns on his face. He Aidan smooths it away after a deep breath. "I know that when I work you over, I like you being a blank slate."

"We'll make something work," Kyle promises.

"I suppose this is a good time for me to remind you that at the end of the month I'm chaperoning a spring break trip."

Oh, right.

When Aidan first brought it up, Kyle made the required jokes about beaches and margaritas, but it turns out Aidan's going on an *educational* trip. He and one of the history professors are taking a group of students to Italy to study Roman architecture and art.

"Italy's a lot farther away than Madison," Kyle says.

"Your conference is in *Wisconsin*?" Aidan asks. He shakes his head as if he can't understand why.

"It's not so bad." Now the important conversations are over, Kyle nudges Aidan's foot with his. "Hurry up and eat, it's time to focus on the present instead of the future."

Aidan grins as he decides to cut his chicken into even smaller pieces.

Kyle should've known better than to try to rush him. "I'll go jerk off on my own."

Aidan looks amused by the threat. "If you'd like, but I can promise it won't be as satisfying as my plans for you tonight."

Kyle groans and decides to start the dishes.

Apparently, Aidan isn't committed to teasing, because it doesn't take him long to join Kyle at the sink. He bumps Kyle's hip with his own as he says, "I'll take care of the dishes. Go get your cuffs."

He grins, unable to help the immediate reaction. Aidan's smile is softer, pleased, and he holds Kyle still for a brief kiss before sending him on his way.

When Kyle returns, Aidan nods toward the living room. "Couch."

Kyle sits on the couch, his cuffs in his lap as he waits. Anticipation makes it difficult for him to slip through. Tonight will be a rare scene where Kyle doesn't know what's going to happen. Usually, the day or two before, they'll talk through a scene, sometimes generally, sometimes more specifically. Even if there isn't always a step-by-step plan, Kyle knows the outline of it.

Tonight, he doesn't know anything.

It'll be his choice to offer his cuffs to Aidan and after that, Aidan will make all the decisions for the night.

A month or two ago, it might've given him pause, and, honestly, Aidan probably would've put his foot down. He's wary of having too much control, something left over from his last relationship, a sub who was new to the scene and wasn't as comfortable saying no as Aidan thought he was.

But this is a different relationship than that. It's been weeks of them establishing the trust they need for this kind of scene. They know each other well enough that both avoid major hard limits, and they've gotten better at reading each other in scene. More importantly, Aidan knows Kyle will speak up if he doesn't like the direction a scene is headed in.

Aidan wanders in from the kitchen, wiping his hands off on Kyle's sweatpants.

"There are dish towels," Kyle points out.

Aidan shrugs.

Once Aidan's within reach, Kyle snags the hem of his shirt and tugs him closer. Aidan, apparently feeling indulgent, allows himself to be pulled down onto Kyle's lap. If his cuffs were already on, then Kyle would tilt his head looking or a kiss or use his words and ask for one, but since they aren't, he pulls Aidan in for the kiss he wants.

Too soon, Aidan pulls back. He plants a hand on Kyle's chest to keep him from following and smiles when Kyle tries anyway.

"We can make out on the couch all night," Aidan offers. His fingers trace the line of Kyle's jaw from his right ear to the curve of his chin. When he's finished, he tips Kyle's head up to make sure he's paying attention. "Or, I can put your cuffs on."

Kyle dips his head to press a kiss to the pads of Aidan's fingers. "Cuffs," he answers. It's an easy choice. And, if he's lucky, he'll end up with his cuffs *and* kissing.

Once his cuffs are secured around his wrists, they switch so it's Aidan sitting on the couch. He pats his lap and shakes his head when Kyle tries to straddle him. *Maybe there won't be kissing*, Kyle thinks as he sits so his back is against Aidan's chest.

Aidan rests a hand on Kyle's hip and squeezes, a silent signal to stay still. With his other hand, he picks up the remote and turns the TV on. He flips channels until he finds *A New Hope*. Luke is searching for R2-D2, and this is classic but, "I have this on DVD. *And* VHS. We could watch from the beginning and without commercials."

"We could," Aidan agrees. He turns the volume down which makes Kyle's frown deepen. He has a lot of opinions on *Star Wars*, from the proper order to watch the movies in, to the proper volume they should be listened to.

He eyes the remote. Aidan hasn't *told* him to stay still.

"Arms around my neck," Aidan says.

He doesn't sound disappointed, but Kyle feels chastised anyway. His stomach dips, disappointed in himself. It isn't a full swoop, the kind that leaves him nauseated and hanging his head, but he isn't being his best right now.

He raises his arms above his head and loops them behind Aidan's neck. He holds his hands in a loose grip, his fingers curled through the rings in his cuffs. Touching his cuffs reminds him why he's here and what they're doing. He trusts Aidan. He doesn't know what game he's playing, but he knows it'll be one he likes. He just has to be patient.

"Let me know if it becomes uncomfortable," Aidan says. His tone is mild, but there's no mistaking it for an order.

Kyle nods and then shifts a little to make this a position he can hold for a while. He bends his elbows so his arms won't grow stiff. He slouches against Aidan's chest, his head resting next to Aidan's so he won't end up with a mouthful of Kyle's hair. He parts his legs, the inside of his knees touching the outside of Aidan's.

It doesn't take him to be caught up in the movie again, and it's a surprise when, instead of flowing into the next scene, a car commercial pops up on screen.

"We could be watching this without commercials," Kyle reminds him.

"This is your favorite movie. I wouldn't want to distract you during it."

Aidan spreads his legs, spreading Kyle's with them until Kyle's pants are stretched to their limit. With his arms around Aidan's neck and his legs splayed wide, Kyle's on display. The knowledge hits him with a sharp gasp, his breath catching then whooshing out all at once.

Aidan laughs, low and warm against his ear. It makes a blush rise up Kyle's neck and into his cheeks. "You look good like this." His skims his hands from Kyle's collarbone down the long, bowed line of Kyle's chest, all the way to his thighs. He nudges them another fraction of an inch apart.

His chest rises and falls, his breath coming fast even though Aidan's barely touched him. And, with Kyle's clothes still on, it isn't so much a touch as a press of skin against fabric.

With Kyle's body open like this, Aidan could do a dozen different things. He could slip his hands under Kyle's shirt or pop the button on Kyle's jeans to pull out his cock.

Or he could leave his hands on Kyle's thighs, a steady, warm touch, which is apparently what he's decided to do. His palms rest high on Kyle's legs, almost where Kyle wants the touch. If he asks nicely, will Aidan slide his hands up another inch?

"Your movie's back on," Aidan tells him.

It's a surprise to see that it is, and he frowns as he realizes he missed the opening of the scene. He almost asks Aidan to rewind, but he doesn't want to give Aidan the satisfaction of knowing he's distracted Kyle.

He's pretty sure he already knows, but Kyle has his pride to protect.

At the next commercial break, Aidan runs his hands up and down Kyle's thighs, a heavy, possessive touch that makes Kyle want to squirm. He holds still, though, even as Aidan's hands purposefully avoid even an incidental touch to Kyle's dick.

He *knows* Aidan won't touch him there and yet, every time his hands sweep up, Kyle goes completely still, breath held, *waiting*, only for Aidan to slide his hands back down. It's the kind of anticipation then denial that winds him tighter and tighter.

He misses the beginning of the next scene too.

He watches, half-hard, and tries to focus on the movie instead of wondering where Aidan will touch him next once they reach a commercial break. He's actually looking forward to the next pause in the move which feels like blasphemy.

When it finally cuts to commercial, Aidan runs his hands up Kyle's chest this time, fingers circling Kyle's nipples but never touching them. Kyle squirms, wanting more. He's somewhat pacified when he feels the hard line of Aidan's cock. At least they're both being teased, even if Aidan's better at holding out than Kyle is.

"Do you want to know the plan for tonight?" Aidan nips at Kyle's neck. When he tilts his head to give Aidan better access, he can feel the curve of Aidan's smile against his skin.

"Yes. Please."

"I'm going to touch you until the movie is over," Aidan tells him. "It'll never quite be the way you want it because I like seeing you desperate. I like how you wriggle and pant and beg for it with every moment of your body."

Fuck, Kyle thinks, even as he presses back into Aidan, proving his point.

"Once the movie is over, I'm going to put you on your knees and you're going to blow me."

Kyle is completely on board with this plan. He turns his head, looking for a kiss. He's only given a brief one against the corner of his mouth which does nothing to satisfy the need growing inside him. Aidan drops his hands to Kyle's hips to hold him still as Aidan grinds up against him.

He wants to make me desperate, Kyle remembers. And he won't give me what I want until the end.

"And after all that," Aidan says, because apparently, he's still not done, "I'm going to jerk you off. It's a good plan, isn't it?"

Kyle nods.

"That'll do for now, but later I'll want words. You'll thank me for fucking your mouth then you'll thank me for my hand on your cock."

Kyle nods again, knowing Aidan can feel it.

"Good. Now, watch your movie."

Aidan continues to tease him by running his hands over Kyle's body during commercial breaks. Sometimes, he touches him for a reaction. Sometimes, he splays a hand against Kyle's stomach to feel his muscles quiver with the strength of holding still or he'll rest a hand on Kyle's chest to feel it rise and fall, too fast for Kyle to be calm.

Everything is a build-up to *more*, and with each commercial break, Kyle's afraid he won't last through the entire movie. He's sweating, the small of his back and his hairline, and his face is flushed, and his dick aches with the need for relief.

Then, as a commercial for insurance ends and *Star Wars* comes back on, Aidan slips two fingers into Kyle's mouth.

"Keep still," Aidan tells him.

He doesn't suck, doesn't lick, doesn't even breathe until his lungs burn, reminding him he kind of needs to do that last one. Tears sting the corners of his eyes and he whines around Aidan's fingers because he wants more.

He loses track of the movie.

He can't split his attention between Aidan and the screen or he'll slip up. Being still means he can't lick between Aidan's fingers. He can't pull back to press kisses against the tips. He has to stay where he is and wait for the next commercial break.

"Show me you want it," Aidan says.

The TV's back on a commercial, and Kyle gratefully sucks on Aidan's fingers, hollowing his cheeks, and giving a preview of what he'll do as soon as the movie's over. He'd do it now, slide to his knees and suck Aidan's cock if he was given permission.

He shamelessly rubs his ass against Aidan's cock, and he's halfway to coming just with the feel of Aidan's hard-on and the two fingers in his mouth. Maybe it's something he should be ashamed of, how easy he is for this, for *Aidan*. But he's never been ashamed of the things he likes, and he doesn't see why he should start now.

Aidan presses his fingers down on Kyle's tongue and says, "Stop."

Kyle whines, the sound muffled by Aidan's fingers. He makes another small sound when Aidan's free hand drops to his crotch. He's hard in his jeans, dick trapped against unforgiving denim, and the press of Aidan's hand is both too much and not enough. He wants to tell Aidan he doesn't need to do this. He doesn't need to slide his fingers in Kyle's mouth and palm Kyle through his jeans as if he wants Kyle to be conditioned to get hard when there's something in his mouth. He managed to get there all on his own.

He tangles his hands in Aidan's hair, desperate for some kind of anchor. All he can focus on are the different places Aidan's touching him and how none of them are enough.

Aidan kisses his neck and murmurs reassurances that Kyle clings to until the next commercial break.

"Please," Kyle begs, the word garbled and near unintelligible around Aidan's fingers.

Aidan slips his fingers free. "What was that?"

"Please," Kyle repeats. He turns his face into Aidan's, surprised when he feels dampness against his cheeks. He blinks back a fresh set of tears and nuzzles Aidan's cheek. "Please, let me blow you."

"Hmm," Aidan says as if he's considering it. As if he might say no.

Kyle's hands tighten in his hair. "*Please.* I need your cock in my mouth. You can tease me once I'm on my knees, but please. Let me have it."

"Look at you begging so nicely," Aidan says. He wipes the tears from Kyle's cheeks. "If you want my cock so badly then you're going to work for it."

Kyle nods, desperate and eager and willing to do anything Aidan asks him.

"Okay." Aidan pets Kyle's sides, soothing. He keeps up the gentle touch until Kyle settles, no longer trembling. He presses a kiss to Kyle's cheek and says, "Grab a pillow and you can get on your knees."

"Thank you," Kyle says.

Aidan's hands squeeze his sides, holding him still for a moment before he takes a deep breath. As soon as he lets Kyle go, he grabs a pillow and drops it between Aidan's legs. He falls onto it with a soft thud, glad he didn't have far to go. He curls his hands around Aidan's knees because he needs to touch, but he isn't sure what's allowed.

He lifts his gaze to Aidan's face and hopes he looks sufficiently desperate because he's not sure he has words right now.

Aidan smiles, fond, as he shoves his pants and his boxers down to his knees. "You can do the rest."

Kyle pulls Aidan's clothes the rest of the way off and tosses them behind him. Then he pushes Aidan's knees apart and moves into the space there. Aidan's hard cock curves up toward his stomach. Kyle starts to lean forward before he glances up, making sure it's okay.

"Go ahead," Aidan says, "but it's just like with my fingers. You can rest it on your tongue but nothing more."

Kyle obediently takes Aidan's cock into his mouth and closes his eyes. His entire body relaxes and his mind settles with the familiar weight on his tongue. The insistent need that's been hammering under his skin fades into something more manageable.

He can do this.

With his eyes closed, he focuses on the smooth skin of Aidan's cock, the heady scent of sweat and arousal. He can't say thank-you like this, but he can show he's thankful by listening and being good.

One of Aidan's hands slides into Kyle's hair. "You can suck me now."

The permission snaps his calm, and Kyle's so eager he chokes himself as he tries to take too much too fast. Aidan laughs, the sound distant, as blood rushes to Kyle's face. He pulls off to press sloppy kisses to the length of Aidan's cock as he catches his breath. Once he feels steady, he tries again.

He goes slower this time, until his mouth is full. It isn't enough. His fingers scrabble against Aidan's legs, needing more but unsure how to get it. He pulls back, sucks in a few harsh breaths, and dives back in again. He's able to take Aidan deeper this time, and the tightness in his chest eases.

Aidan uses two hands in Kyle's hair to pull him off. "The movie's back on," Aidan explains, his voice hoarse.

Kyle rests his forehead against Aidan's thigh and takes several deep breaths. Once his heart doesn't feel like it's going to beat right out of his chest, he closes his eyes and allows himself to drift.

When Aidan tugs on his hair, Kyle's eyes snap open, hopeful but wary.

"Again."

Kyle is more direct this time now he knows he only has a small window before he loses the privilege again. He sucks the tip of Aidan's cock into his mouth so he can taste the welling precome then he flicks his tongue under the head so Aidan will tighten his hands in his hair.

He knows how to make him come from a blowjob, but when he starts pulling out Aidan's favorite tricks, Aidan pulls on his hair, a sharp warning.

"Not until the movie's over," Aidan says.

Kyle glances up, eyes narrowed.

Aidan laughs as he thumbs at the corner of Kyle's mouth, where it's stretched by Aidan's cock. "You told me I could tease you as much as I wanted. You begged for this, remember?"

Kyle narrows his eyes even more, annoyed with himself for his short-sightedness and annoyed with Aidan for talking himself out of an orgasm. People and their fucking self-control.

"Show me how much you love sucking my cock," Aidan says. "I want to hear you enjoy it. I want to see it."

Kyle curls his tongue against the underside of Aidan's dick. He's rewarded with another spurt of precome, and he makes a show of swallowing. He even pulls off to lick his lips. "Like that?"

Aidan's eyes glitter dangerously before he nudges his leg between Kyle's. His shin presses against Kyle's cock. "Like this."

He's caught off guard and Kyle's eyes widen, a protest on his lips, even as his cheeks fill with heat and his dick jerks, *wanting*.

"Show me," Aidan says.

Hot and embarrassed shifts easily into turned on. It doesn't take long for the flush in his cheeks and the clench of his stomach to melt from unsure to *yes* and *please* and *now*.

He rolls his hips and presses the line of his dick against Aidan's leg. After so long of not having any kind of friction it feels good. Almost too good. He kisses the base of Aidan's cock to distract himself from his own, but it doesn't work.

He rolls his hips again, chasing his own pleasure as he licks and sucks his way down to Aidan's balls. He's not allowed to make Aidan come, but there are no rules about himself. He's at the edge sooner than he'd like to admit and, once he's there, he doesn't see a reason to hold himself back.

Aidan wanted to see this. It's the final push he needs to let go. It rocks through him, leaving him breathless and wrung out. He turns to mouth at Aidan's cock as he comes down, needing something to ground him. He feels empty and shaky as if it was over too quickly for something that had been building for so long.

He breathes hard between kisses, and he pauses when he realizes he's panting on Aidan's dick.

Something ugly twists in his stomach, and he glances up, tentative and fragile. He's braced for Aidan to laugh at him but knows it won't be enough. One harsh word and he'll crumble.

Aidan slides his fingers through Kyle's hair and tips his head back so it's easier for him to look up. "You're good," Aidan promises.

It soothes the worst of his fear, but he's still left unsettled. He needs something, but his brain won't work enough to tell him what it is.

"Can you keep my cock warm for me now?" Aidan asks.

Kyle nods. He can do that. He feels loose enough he could probably do it for the rest of the night, not that he wants to. He wants to make Aidan as happy as Aidan's made him.

Aidan's hands guide Kyle forward. He parts his lips so he can catch the tip of Aidan's cock in his mouth and then he slides down the length of it. His eyes slip closed, and he thinks he could easily sink into this headspace.

Then Aidan drops his hands from Kyle's hair, and Kyle makes a small, protesting sound.

Aidan weaves his hands through Kyle's hair again. "Better?"

Kyle nods.

"You're good," Aidan tells him again.

Kyle takes a deep breath and believes him.

He kneels there, mind and body finally quiet, until the movie ends. The TV clicks off, the background voices gone, and it's only him and Aidan in the room. He slowly opens his eyes as if he's emerging from a languid nap, and Aidan's looking down at him. His smile is soft and he cards his fingers through Kyle's hair with none of the urgency he'd expect.

"You've been so good for me," Aidan says.

He scratches his fingers against Kyle's scalp, and he makes a noise closer to a purr than anything human. Aidan groans, which is when Kyle remembers, *oh, I still have his cock in my mouth.*

"I want to come on your face," Aidan says. "Will you let me?"

Kyle nods. He doesn't fight Aidan when he pulls Kyle off his cock.

"Close your eyes again," Aidan tells him.

He closes his eyes and tilts his head back. He parts his lips without being asked. He won't be able to swallow, but at least he'll have a taste.

"You look so good kneeling here at my feet with your mouth open, waiting and *wanting*. I love how you beg without a single word."

He would talk if he thought it's what Aidan wanted. He'd tell Aidan how he wants Aidan in every way he can have him. He'd say he knows Aidan feels the same way and it's the reason why he's as open and trusting as he is. He knows Aidan wants him as badly as Kyle wants Aidan, and it gives him the courage to push his limits.

It's the best kind of feedback loop, and he wants to see where it will take them. Will they move in together and start to scene more? Kyle doesn't want to wear his cuffs all the time, but he'd like to be Aidan's all the time. He wants his place to be on his knees for Aidan, tucked under Aidan's arm on the couch, or cuddled close to him in bed. He wants his place to be at Aidan's side, and he wants Aidan's place to be at his.

Kyle wants to pull his bottom lip between his teeth to catch his thoughts before they all spill out of his mouth. But Aidan doesn't like it when he does that so he flicks his tongue over his lips instead.

"Fuck," Aidan groans.

It's Kyle's only warning before come splatters across his cheeks and his lips. He keeps his eyes closed as Aidan rubs his come into Kyle's skin, marking him. Kyle's next breath is shaky, want and need colliding painfully inside his chest, squeezing his heart. He reaches his hands out, desperate, but he doesn't know what for.

Aidan holds Kyle's face between his hands. He presses his lips to Kyle's, kissing the taste of his own come from them. Kyle leans up into the kiss and tries to chase Aidan's mouth as he pulls back.

Aidan's thumbs sweep across Kyle's cheeks. "Open your eyes."

Kyle's eyes flutter open.

"Up here."

Kyle straddles Aidan's lap, glad to be close to him again. He enjoys being on his knees, but he enjoys this too. If Aidan wants to wrap his arms around Kyle and sit like this for a while, Kyle wouldn't mind. Some cuddling on the couch, a shower, then some cuddling in bed.

It sounds like the perfect end to their evening.

Aidan pops the button on Kyle's jeans and drags the zipper down. These pants are loose enough Aidan can push his jeans and briefs down so that Kyle isn't trapped in his come-damp clothes anymore.

It's good until Aidan reaches into the end table drawer to pull out the bottle of lube Kyle keeps there.

"I can't," Kyle says as Aidan squeezes a line of lube down Kyle's soft dick. "It's too soon."

"What did I tell you we were doing tonight?" Aidan asks. He only uses the tips of two fingers to spread the lube, but even that light touch borders on too much.

It's hard to think with Aidan touching him but... "Oh. I was going to blow you then you were going to jerk me off."

"Mmm," Aidan agrees. He wraps a loose fist around Kyle's dick, and Kyle tries to pull away. Aidan tuts his tongue. "Are you saying I shouldn't keep my promises?"

"You knew," Kyle accuses. "When you told me to get off, you had this planned."

"You knew too. I told you in the beginning."

Aidan smiles, proud of himself. He strokes Kyle with a slow, even rhythm as if he's trying to coax him back to hardness. It's the exact kind of too much that he likes, even as he hates it. He grows hard until Aidan's patience touch. Soon, he doesn't know whether he wants more or wants it to stop. He pushes into Aidan's fist and then tries to pull away until he's writhing on Aidan's lap.

His hair is sweaty and sticking to his forehead. His cheeks are flushed, and he can't seem to drag in enough oxygen with each breath. Aidan, however, is completely composed. He watches every jerk of Kyle's hips and wipes the tears from Kyle's cheeks when he grows overwhelmed by everything he's feeling.

"I didn't tell you had to get off earlier," Aidan says. "I gave you the choice."

Which means Kyle brought this on himself. His spunk is still drying from his first orgasm as Aidan wrings a second out of him. He's overheated and oversensitive, but he still crowds close to Aidan, allowing the other man to do what he wants. No wonder he looks so pleased.

"I let you come," Aidan continues, his voice serving as an anchor to keep Kyle from drifting away with his thoughts. "And I'm going to let you again. That's nice of me, isn't it?"

"Fuck," Kyle breathes as he realizes what Aidan wants. He curls his fingers around Aidan's shoulders, looking for some kind of purchase. His cock pulses, precome dribbling out. Aidan collects it on his thumb and smears it around the head of Kyle's cock.

Kyle shivers and groans, and he wants to drop his head to Aidan's shoulders, but he doesn't. He holds himself up, looks in Aidan's eyes as he says, "Thank you.

Thank you for letting me come twice in one night. Thank you for being nice to me, for being *good* to me. Thank yo— oh. *Oh*."

A twist of Aidan's wrist and he comes again, his gaze locked on Aidan's. It's pain edged with pleasure or pleasure edged with pain. It's a hot spark of *something* and it doesn't last long enough. Now, he drops his head to Aidan's shoulder, breathing heavily. He whines when Aidan eases his hand off his cock. The air in the room is too chilly after the heat of Aidan's hand, but if Aidan touches him again, he might scream.

"You're good," Aidan promises. He pets Kyle's hair, soothing. "You were so good for me."

"You fucking ruined *Star Wars*," Kyle mumbles. Now he's slumped forward and given his weight to Aidan, he doesn't want to take it back. Aidan can carry him to bed or they can sleep here. He isn't picky.

"You didn't enjoy yourself?" Aidan asks, teasing. "Maybe you didn't get enough."

His hand creeps downward, and Kyle grabs his wrist. "I got plenty."

Aidan laughs and wiggles his fingers but doesn't make any real effort to break Kyle's grip. "Are you sure?"

"Positive."

"I never thought I'd hear you beg *not* to have an orgasm." He pauses, thoughtful. "We should try that sometime."

"Sadist."

"Little bit. But you like it."

"I do."

Kyle lifts his head off Aidan's shoulder so they can kiss.

It takes them a long time to get off the couch.

Chapter Four

"THE EXPO IS a go," Kyle announces as he enters Jenny and Charlotte's apartment. The two grocery bags hanging off his left arm have slowly been cutting off his circulation.

"Oh, thank fuck," Jenny says, a more enthusiastic response than Kyle had been expecting.

It makes more sense when he sees the open cookbook on her island counter and the scattered ingredients surrounding it. Her enthusiasm isn't for his announcement but rather her hope that he'll rescue her from making dinner.

"You still have this?" he asks, nudging the book aside so there's room for him to set his bags down.

"It was a gift from my mother which means I can't throw it away. And, if there's ever a fire, it has to be the first thing I grab to bring out of the apartment with me."

Kyle laughs and glances at the celery stalks and clementines at Jenny's elbow. "Do I even want to know?"

"The celery was for dinner," Charlotte answers. She emerges from their bedroom in a sweater big enough for her to tuck her hands inside the sleeves. "The clementines are because *some people*—" she gives Jenny a stern look "—snack while making dinner, and it becomes a problem when she eats our cooking ingredients."

"Tell me about it," Kyle says. "Every time I make cookies, I only end up with half the number I'm supposed to because she can't keep her fingers out of the bowl."

"Clearly the solution is to make a double batch." Jenny shuffles around the counter until she can rest her chin on Kyle's shoulder and peer into his bags. "What are you making us?"

"Bacon-and-cheese-stuffed potatoes and some kind of chicken."

"Or no chicken," Jenny says. "Bacon counts as protein."

"Definitely chicken. Broccoli too."

"Ugh." She digs her chin into Kyle's shoulder.

"Yes, how dare I include a vegetable with our meal."

He laughs as he nudges her away so he can start dinner prep. He's always loved to cook, even when he was illegally using a hotplate in college to try to make something more palatable than microwave ramen in his shoebox of a dorm room. Cooking is better when he does it for more than just himself, though.

He cooks for Jenny and Charlotte a couple of times a week and for Aidan as much as he can. It settles the part of him that wants to make sure everyone he's close to is well taken care of.

"If you're so anti-vegetable then why is there celery on the counter?"

"Charlotte said we needed to have a vegetable at dinner. We were going to slap on some peanut butter for protein and some raisins for fruit and—bam, balanced meal."

Kyle can't keep the horrified look off his face. "First of all, that's a snack, not a meal. Second of all, it's a snack for *kids*. It's the kind of thing I'd pack for myself in grade school."

He'd been in charge of his own school lunch when he was younger. His mom worked full-time and his dad didn't know anything about cooking, so his options were to stand forever in a line for food he didn't even want at the cafeteria or to make things for himself.

When his mom remarried, Kyle gained two brothers and a sister, and he made lunch for them too. By then, he'd grown beyond peanut butter and jelly slapped on two slices of bread. He was making turkey sandwiches with tomato and guacamole and homemade dessert instead of cookies bought at the store.

He still remembers his stepdad awkwardly approaching him a couple of weeks after they were all living in the same house and asking if Kyle could make lunch for him too. He was braced for the "I'm not your dad, but I could be" talk or the "let's all get along for the sake for your mother" speech, and he'd been thrown by the request.

Then pleased.

It was his stepdad who gave him his first cookbook, battered and stained, that had belonged to Brian's mother before she gave it to Brian. The pages were kept in a three-ring binder, the margins of the recipes filled with handwritten notes.

Kyle and Brian made dinner together almost every night, simple things during the week then experimenting on the weekend when they had the time. Their experiments sometimes ended with having to order pizza, but sometimes they landed on new family recipes like Cheez-It breaded chicken.

They still cook together when Kyle's home for a visit, and they send each other new recipes they've tried. He has a three-ring binder in his kitchen with photocopied pages of Brian's cookbook. In the back, he's added the new recipes they've discovered over the years. There's one for chili he's been meaning to try. He'll break it out the next time they have a cold snap.

"Wait," Jenny says, and Kyle pauses, his fork poised over a potato. "Did you say you're coming to the Expo?"

Kyle and Charlotte roll their eyes and then laugh when they catch the other doing it.

"Stop that," Jenny says. "I was distracted by food when you came in. I'm focused now."

Kyle stabs each of the potatoes with a fork. "Yes, I'm going to the Expo."

"Awesome. I'll email the guy. We need to plan what I'm doing with you. Is Aidan coming with us?"

"He has finals that week. He'll be stuck here while we're partying in Madison."

"Does he want to sit in on our brainstorming session?"

"Doubtful but I'll ask."

He rubs the potatoes in butter and salt and a sprinkling of pepper before wrapping them in foil and sticking them in the oven.

"Where's he now?" Charlotte asks. "You can invite him over for dinner. Unless you don't spend time together out of scenes."

Kyle's certainly had scene partners who he saw in scene and that was it. Their interests lined up in the bedroom, or club room, and not as much outside of it. Aidan's different. Kyle would intertwine every aspect of their lives if he could.

Jenny pulls Kyle's phone out of his back pocket and punches in his passcode. She finds Aidan in his contacts and hits call before holding the phone up to Kyle's ear as Kyle moves to the next stage of dinner prep; the chicken.

"Hello?" Aidan asks when he answers, curious, as if he doesn't know why Kyle's calling him.

"Hey, I'm making dinner right now for Jenny and Charlotte. You want to join us? There's plenty of food for a fourth."

He marinates the chicken, a simple Italian dressing glaze because the real masterpiece of this meal is the potatoes.

"We'd love to have you," Jenny adds and grins when Kyle can't do anything because his hands are covered in salad dressing and raw chicken.

Kyle glares at her before asking, "Are you still at school?"

"I am. I was planning to stay and grade, but dinner with friends sounds better. I have to stop at home, but I can be there in forty minutes. Half an hour if I rush."

"I haven't even put the chicken in the oven yet." He'll need to marinate some more chicken and prepare more potatoes. "Do you want to invite Ritchie and Caroline if they're home?"

"I can do that. It'll double the people there. Can we bring anything?"

"Beer," Jenny answers, "and board games if you have them. No Monopoly. Kyle and I almost ended our friendship over a game and it's been banned ever since."

Aidan laughs. "Beer and anything but Monopoly. I can handle that."

THEY BRING MORE than just beer and a few games. Aidan has a case of beer and Caroline has a couple of games, but Ritchie is carrying a whole cheesecake platter.

"Hello, new best friend," Jenny says, lifting the platter out of Ritchie's hands. She strokes the top before glancing at its previous owner. "I'm Jenny."

"Ritchie."

"My girlfriend's around here somewhere," Jenny says as she carries the cheesecake to the counter. "I don't know where she went, but I know how to summon her."

Jenny winks at Ritchie before she pops the plastic covering off the cheesecake. The plastic squeaks against itself and Charlotte comes down the hall with a mild, "Not before dinner, you'll ruin your appetite." She smiles at their guests. "I'm Charlotte. Welcome to our apartment."

Kyle slides the cheesecake out from Jenny's hands and puts it in the fridge before anyone can give in to temptation. "Jenny, Charlotte, meet Ritchie and Caroline. They work with Aidan."

"I can talk about compost for days," Ritchie says.

Caroline pats his arm. "They don't care about that, babe. I coach women's soccer."

"Sports?" Jenny looks skeptical. "One time in gym class, I kicked the ball backward into my own goal."

Kyle laughs as he checks on dinner. He's heard this story plenty of times; hell, he was there when it happened, and he lets the familiar tale wash over him as Jenny settles their company in the living room.

Aidan makes space for the beer in the fridge and then waits for Kyle to close the oven before he steps in to give him a quick kiss.

"Almost done," Kyle says.

"I'll set the table then. It smells good."

"That's probably the bacon."

Aidan opens the cabinet next to the refrigerator and stares, baffled, at the brightly colored boxes of cereal.

"This isn't my apartment," Kyle reminds him. "Plates are over there." He tilts his head to indicate the cabinets to the left of the microwave.

"Your apartments have the same layout, and you don't organize them the same way?" Aidan drops another kiss to Kyle's cheek as he shuffles past him.

"Jenny claims she's 'maintaining her individuality.' I call it being a pain in the ass."

Aidan laughs as he pulls a stack of plates down from the cabinet.

"I hear you badmouthing me!" Jenny calls from the couch. "The apartment's open complex which means no fucking walls to hide what you're saying."

"Your plates are in the wrong place!" Aidan shouts back, laughing again as she holds up a middle finger.

"We have *guests*," Charlotte says.

"I coach a collegiate sports team," Caroline says. "I've heard women swear before. You don't need to censor yourself on my behalf."

"Charlotte works at the library," Jenny explains. "She's used to indoor voices and polite words."

"Then I come home to my loud, foul-mouthed girlfriend." Charlotte sighs, aiming for long-suffering, but hits closer to fond.

"You love my mouth," Jenny says, and Kyle can hear the smirk in her tone.

"Let's keep it PG over there on the couch, eh?" Kyle asks.

"How close is dinner to being done?" Jenny asks.

"Just a couple more minutes."

THE SIX OF them eat dinner together and linger over their beers before Charlotte asks, "Time for Stage Two of the evening?"

"Aidan and I get to pick the first game," Kyle says.

"Charlotte and I will do the dishes then," Jenny says, "Ritchie and Caroline, you know where the couch is. You can relax."

"That hardly seems fair," Caroline protests.

Jenny takes her plate before she can do anything about it. Kyle stacks his and Aidan's before handing them over.

"I cooked, so I don't do the dishes," Kyle explains. "And you're guests, so you don't do the dishes. Next time we'll do something at your place."

"Bi-weekly couples' night?" Charlotte asks.

Ritchie pauses as he stands up from the table. He looks from Aidan to Kyle and then back to Aidan. "Wait, you're together?"

Jenny has to set the plate down on the counter so she doesn't drop them as she starts laughing. Charlotte covers her mouth to hide her smile.

"Babe," Caroline groans.

"We're together," Aidan answers.

Kyle knows Ritchie isn't clued in enough to pick up on a lot of social signals. The first time they met, he thought Kyle was the new faculty member even though the semester hadn't switched over yet. All the times he's dropped by unannounced make more sense if he didn't realize Kyle and Aidan were together, but, honestly, Kyle doesn't think they're that subtle.

Ritchie looks as if his entire world is reorienting itself. "I thought you just really liked breakfast."

"Breakfast buddies," Jenny giggles. "Like gal pals but with French toast involved."

"How many morning-afters have you interrupted?" Caroline asks. To Kyle she says, "I'm so sorry."

"We were wearing clothes. No harm done."

"Well, I would've figured it out if you were naked," Ritchie says.

Kyle grins as he reaches for Aidan's hand. "Let's pick a game. I'm leaning toward Taboo because Jenny always tries to go through a whole round without breathing and her face gets super red."

"Fuck you," Jenny says.

"Nah, I'll let Aidan handle that. You know, since we're together."

"I'm never going to live this down," Ritchie says. He doesn't look too bothered by it. "But if you're together then you should come to some of our faculty stuff."

"*Yes*," Caroline agrees as they follow Aidan and Kyle into the living room. "I could use someone to talk to. I go to the Senior Project Symposium to support his students and my athletes, but most of what they study goes right over my head."

Kyle's "yes" is on the tip of his tongue before he glances at Aidan. They are together, but what Caroline's talking about sounds like dating activities, and they're together in a sex sense. He's not sure about *dating*. He wouldn't mind it, but he doesn't want to cross any boundaries if Aidan isn't comfortable with it.

"I'd love for you to come," Aidan says. "There's an annual art showing for all the art majors, whether they're seniors or not. I think you'd like it. They even display fake art."

Kyle laughs and tugs him down onto the two-person couch. "I'll have you know that fake art pays my bills."

"There's a story here," Caroline says as she and Ritchie sit on the bigger couch.

"I'm a freelance graphic designer and when I heard Aidan was an art history professor I was nervous because sometimes academics have a bias toward us common, modern folks. But then I actually talked to him and he turned out to be an okay guy."

Aidan gently elbows him. "Just okay?"

"You've grown on me. You're probably at cool guy level now."

Aidan leans forward to look at the stack of games on the coffee table. "All right, *cool guy*, what're we playing first?"

Kyle rummages through the games under the table until he emerges with a battered Taboo box.

"Ritchie sucks at this game," Caroline says.

"Do not," Ritchie protests.

"He won't skip cards," Caroline tells Kyle, "but he never makes references I understand."

"No couple advantage for you?"

"Sadly, no." Caroline taps Blurt. "This is more my speed; a bunch of people trying to yell louder than each other."

"That's not really—" Ritchie begins. At Caroline's look, he shrugs and says, "Close enough, I suppose."

Kyle tries not to stare too much as they have an entire argument then apology then make up in just the scrunch of their eyebrows and quirk of their lips. He supposes that's what happens after being in a relationship with someone for so long.

He spares a glance at Aidan and wonders if they'll ever reach that stage. Apparently, they're at the stage where they go to each other's work functions. Will Kyle need a fleece vest for this? Aidan has the market cornered on tweed and elbow pads which means Kyle needs his own signature look. Fleece vests could totally be his thing.

"Ready to lose?" Jenny asks, dropping onto Kyle's lap.

He grunts and dumps her on the floor.

"Rude." She snatches the buzzer and buzzes it right in his ear.

Charlotte plucks the buzzer from her hands before she can do any more damage with it.

They settle down enough to play and make it through a few rounds before they switch to Blurt. They play a more sedate game of Skip-Bo afterward and then break out the cheesecake. By the end of the night, Kyle leans heavily against Aidan's side.

Charlotte and Jenny are holding hands, and Caroline picks at the remains of Ritchie's cheesecake. It makes Kyle wish that after this they would all go their separate ways; Jenny and Charlotte at home, Ritchie and Caroline at home, and Aidan and Kyle at home.

But Aidan has early classes tomorrow and it means Aidan's staying at his house and Kyle's staying in his apartment. They aren't the kind of couple who spends the night just to share a bed. Of course, before tonight they weren't the kind of couple who has dinner and board game nights with other couples.

"We should head out," Caroline says once she's finished Ritchie's cheesecake. "I have early morning conditioning."

"Dumb question," Jenny says, "but isn't soccer played in the fall?"

"We have a full fall season and a partial spring season to make sure our players stay in shape and out of trouble. Nothing curbs partying like six a.m. practices." She looks over at Aidan. "Are you staying longer?"

"I can give you a ride," Kyle offers.

"You don't have to," Aidan says.

Kyle isn't sure if Aidan's saying it to be polite or because he doesn't want Kyle to give him a ride home. Selfishly, Kyle wants some time alone with Aidan, and he definitely wants a few goodnight kisses. If Aidan wants his space, though, then Kyle can back off. He's not sure how to convey all of that in a look.

"That would be nice, thank you," Aidan says.

They head for Kyle's apartment, Aidan's pace slowing as they approach. He steps through the door but looks apprehensive, *this* look one Kyle's able to read.

"I'm not trapping you here," Kyle promises. "I really will drive you home. I guess I shouldn't pack a bag then."

"I have class in the morning."

"I know, it would just be to sleep." Kyle shoves his hands into his pockets so he doesn't fidget. "It's fine. I'll drop you off. Let me grab my keys."

He's turning away when Aidan catches his arm. "I wasn't saying no."

You weren't saying yes either, and that's the important one. "It's not what we do." Kyle summons a smile he doesn't feel. They've never shared a bed unless they scened together first. Kyle might want to push for more, but it doesn't mean Aidan does.

"Pack a bag," Aidan says. "I won't say no to waking up next to you."

"Sap," Kyle says. He leans in for a lingering kiss before heading down the hall to his bedroom.

He packs a simple overnight bag—pajamas, a change of clothes for tomorrow, and his toiletry bag. His cuffs stay here.

Look at me, giddy at the thought of not having sex. What kind of upside-down world have I found myself in?

Chapter Five

THEY SPEND ALMOST every night together leading up to Aidan's spring break trip. Aidan will crash at Kyle's apartment when he has late classes, and they'll have a leisurely morning with breakfast and sometimes a shared shower. On the nights they stay at Aidan's, they'll have dinner with Caroline and Ritchie more often than not.

On those nights, they go to bed early so they can have a long make-out session before Aidan insists that he needs to go to bed, "for real this time."

It means he's unprepared to sleep alone in his bed the first night Aidan's gone.

It takes him ten minutes of flipping from side to side to realize this won't work. It takes another five minutes for him to collect all his extra pillows and create a human-shaped lump to sleep next to. It isn't as good as sleeping next to Aidan. His pillows don't wrap an arm around his waist or press kisses to the back of his neck, but it's better than nothing.

In the morning, he takes a picture of his pillows and sends it via Skype to Aidan.

You've spoiled me, he types.

He makes breakfast, eggs with broccoli and ham, and wonders if he should invite Jenny over. Breakfast is better when it's shared, and she never turns down a meal made by someone else.

Skype dings with a message as he's pulling more eggs out of the fridge.

Spoiling you is my job, Aidan types back.

Kyle grins and settles in front of his computer with his plate. *Consider it a job well done.*

How's Italy?

Beautiful.

Aidan sends a few pictures from out his window. Everything is tucked close together, apartments and shops. Kyle can't help but find it more claustrophobic than beautiful. When he looks out of his window, there are a few other apartment buildings, but there's also a marsh with a black fence around it and, beyond it, there's a cluster of trees, too small to be called a forest.

He's not sure how he'd fare in a *city.*

We're headed to our first museum, Aidan tells him. *I'll send you pictures when we get back.*

Have fun!

Kyle exits out of Skype before he says something like *I miss you.* It's only been one day, and Aidan's whole trip is a week. They'll be fine spending seven days apart.

Still, he picks up his phone and texts Jenny an invite to breakfast.

BY DAY THREE, Kyle has a pattern. He wakes up, works out, eats breakfast then brings his computer to Jenny's apartment, and they work side by side until lunch. After lunch, Kyle returns to his own apartment to get in another hour or two of work before Aidan Skypes him.

So far, Aidan's sent a lot of pictures of food and wine racks. Selfies are rare which makes it even more unfair that they don't video chat. Facebook is where the bulk of the pictures are. Kyle spends dinner scrolling through three days' worth of them. He links his favorite shots of the statues into their Skype chat.

You're looking at naked men who aren't me? My feelings are hurt.

You're not as funny as you think you are, Aidan replies, right away.

Their dicks are small but at least they're hard. One might even say...rock hard.

You. Are. The. Worst.

Lies. Brb.

Kyle studies the last statue he linked a picture to, the Apollo Belvedere, then strips down. It takes him two minutes to find something that will drape appropriately, one of his spare curtains.

Six pictures and several adjustments later, Kyle has a pretty terrible impression of the Apollo Belvedere. He still sends it to Aidan.

There, look at this instead.

There's a long pause, made longer by the "..." bubble that means Aidan is typing a response. Finally, he says, *The presentation is good but the accuracy isn't quite there. 3/10.*

Kyle stares at Aidan's response for a full minute before he says, "He did fucking not," and furiously types back.

Is that how it is?

That's how it is.

Challenge fucking accepted.

KYLE SPENDS THE next few days too busy recreating Roman statues to miss Aidan. He's given a couple of threes and one five for his efforts. Then he's given a zero when he takes a picture of himself lying in bed with his legs spread and the caption, *waiting for Zeus to find me.*

Apparently, Zeus is Greek and not Roman, and Kyle's mistake is so catastrophic that Aidan doesn't even comment on the fact Kyle was naked.

He's pouting at his phone when Jenny barges into his apartment.

Her smile freezes on her face, and her eyes narrow, preparing for a fight. "I can kick his ass even if he's in Rome."

"We're arguing over Greek versus Roman nomenclature," Kyle says.

Aggression melts into confusion. "Sounds nerdy but not worth the sad eyes."

"I sent him naked pictures and he wants to give me a lecture on *nomenclature*." Kyle groans and slouches in his chair. "I think the sex is gone from our relationship."

Jenny laughs at him.

"Seriously," he says. "It's almost been a *week*. He's sharing a room with the other professor on the trip, so there's no Skype sex. He won't even send me dick pics."

"And yet you still talk to him every day." Jenny pokes her head in Kyle's refrigerator. "Do you have any good leftovers?"

"Of course I'm still talking to him. And when he comes home, he's gonna fuck me so hard."

"Ugh. Don't ruin my appetite."

Kyle pushes away from the table and looks around her into the fridge. "Take out the taco soup. I'll make some rice to mix in." He accidentally put too much spice in it, but the rice should soak some of it up. And he has a full tub of sour cream.

"You two are good, though?" Jenny asks as she takes the sturdy Tupperware out of the fridge. "This is your first separation, right?"

"We're good, but distance means I have the space to think about my feelings."

"Oh boy." Jenny hops up on the counter even though he has four barstools on the other side of the island. "Okay, lay it on me."

Kyle rolls his eyes as he pulls a box of rice out of his pantry and hunts down a saucepan. "I like him." He sounds defensive and hates it. He doesn't need to justify his feelings, especially not to Jenny.

"But do you *like* like him?"

"We're not in middle school."

"You're deflecting." Jenny stops swinging her legs. She narrows her eyes, assessing, and Kyle squirms. "Holy shit, you're *deflecting*. You do like him."

"I love him."

Jenny's mouth opens and then closes. She manages a strangled, "*Dude.*"

Kyle shrugs as if he didn't just drop a bombshell on his best friend.

"I'm sorry, I'll be more supportive in a minute. This is not what I was expecting when I came over." She takes a deep breath. "All right, you're in love with him. I probably should've seen this coming. Have you told him?"

Kyle shakes his head then turns to the sink, an excuse not to look at Jenny. He pours four cups of water into the saucepan. He's known since the beginning that Aidan was special. He hadn't realized how special until recently. He's been sitting on the realization, unsure of what to do with it. Telling Jenny seemed safer than telling Aidan. He should've figured she'd want to talk about it.

"Not yet," he answers. "He's in Italy."

"There's no way you figured out you're in love with him this week. Besides, Italy is the perfect time. It's like romantic and shit."

"So I should just Skype him and say 'hey, light some candles, I have something to tell you'?"

"Yes. Exactly. You could even do it minus the candles. I don't understand your obsession."

Candles mark important moments: birthdays, anniversaries, romantic announcements. That's one of the basic rules of life.

"You could always tell him and see if he says it back," Jenny says.

But what if he doesn't? Kyle isn't ready to take that chance yet. "We still have a few months." He doesn't want to jeopardize their arrangement when there's so much time left. He also doesn't want to end up trapped in a dead-end relationship. At the end of this extension, they'll talk. If they're still on the same page then Kyle will ask for something without an end date on it. And if not...well, he's not ready to think about that yet.

"You're going to wait until the last minute? Do you need someone to practice the conversation with? I volunteer Charlotte."

"I figured I'd give him something. I heard somewhere that action speaks louder than words."

"That doesn't mean words aren't good for things like *communication*." Jenny's heels thump against the cabinet. "Wait, what exactly are you giving him?"

Kyle eyes the pot of water as if he can will it to boil faster.

"No way," Jenny says. She slides off the counter so she can plant herself in front of him. It means he has no choice but to face her. "Did you buy a *collar*?"

Kyle regrets everything that's led to this conversation.

"You did! Holy shit!" She touches his shoulders then his cheeks. She has to circle the island before she pulls him in for a hug. "This is huge! Why didn't you lead with this?"

"Ugh."

"Ugh?" She shakes his shoulders. "What do you mean *ugh*?"

"This is why I don't tell you things."

"Because I'm your best and most supportive friend?"

"Because you're getting my hopes up, and I don't know if he'll want it."

Jenny pats his cheeks and kisses his forehead. "Of course he will. He's stupid if he isn't in love with you. How long do I have to keep this a secret for?"

"August."

"It's *March*! Are you sure you don't want to offer him your collar when he gets back from Italy?"

Kyle shakes his head.

"Yeah, you're right. It's a big decision, and I shouldn't rush you. I'm sorry. He'll say yes, though. He'd be an idiot not to."

"Thanks."

Finally, the water boils, and Kyle's able to turn their conversation toward food rather than feelings.

THE NIGHT BEFORE Aidan's due home, Kyle has dinner with Ritchie and Caroline. At first, he thought it would be weird to hang out with Aidan's friends while Aidan isn't here. Caroline thinks he and Aidan are a couple; she doesn't know they started as sex partners, and *Kyle* doesn't know how far out of that territory they've moved.

Jenny told him he was overthinking it and to go to dinner so he went.

"We ordered Italian," Caroline says as she opens the door to her half of the duplex. The house smells like garlic bread and pasta sauce, and Kyle's stomach grumbles. "We're going to take pictures and send them to Aidan. It's Ritchie's idea of a joke."

"If he laughs at Ritchie's jokes after not laughing at mine then we're going to fight."

"You and Aidan or you and Ritchie?"

Kyle closes the door behind him as he follows Caroline into the kitchen. "Both? Both sounds good."

There's a long table in the hallway, covered in pictures. Kyle slows down so he can look at the glimpses of their life Ritchie and Caroline have put on display. There's one of Caroline with her soccer team. The captains are kneeling next to a trophy and everyone else is holding up a single finger.

"That was a good season," Caroline says, following his gaze. "We've lost in the finals twice since." She taps the picture next to it, one of Ritchie elbow-deep in compost. "His idea of a good time."

"You love him anyway."

"I do." She shakes her head as if she can't quite believe it. "Every relationship I've been in, there's been one annoying thing. He's the first person I've loved despite it. That's how I know he's the one." They continue toward the kitchen. "Are you picking Aidan up at the airport tomorrow?"

"Another one of the art history professors is picking him up because his car's still at the school. I'll be here when he comes home."

Caroline pulls the wineglasses out of the cabinet. She turns to grin at him over her shoulder. "So we should postpone our welcome-backs until the day after?"

"Knock before you come over. We might be having breakfast."

"Ha ha," Ritchie says. He pops the lid on an enormous container of pasta.

Caroline sets the glasses on the table and then opens the drawer next to the dishwasher. She frowns as she rifles through it. "Babe, where's the corkscrew? It's not in the miscellaneous kitchen utensil drawer."

"That's because it's in the odds-and-ends drawer."

Caroline opens a drawer on the far end of the counter and pulls out the corkscrew. "But it's a kitchen utensil."

Kyle grins and settles into his chair to play spectator to what sounds like a familiar argument. It ends with Caroline ruffling Ritchie's hair and leaning down for a quick kiss. Kyle loads his plate up with chicken parm and spaghetti and ignores the pang in his chest.

Tomorrow, he'll have Aidan back.

HE SPENDS A good twenty minutes deciding how exactly he wants to welcome Aidan home. Should he linger by the front door so he can kiss Aidan as soon as he walks through? Should he watch by the window so he can help Aidan carry his bags in? Is it time to light some candles? Those are suitably romantic, right?

In the end, he leaves a trail of his clothes from the front door to Aidan's bedroom. He sprawls across Aidan's bed with the sheet draped over him like a toga. Then he pulls out his phone and scrolls through his news feed as he passes the time.

He hears the front door open and tucks his phone away. A few minutes later, Aidan drags his bags into the room and drops them just inside the door. With a grin, Kyle stretches out and props himself up on his elbow.

"I call it *Man Waiting for his Lover's Return*," Kyle says. "What do you think?"

"Ten out of ten," Aidan says. "It's a masterpiece."

Kyle rolls his eyes even as he motions for Aidan to come closer. Smiling indulgently, Aidan shuffles toward the bed. Kyle pushes himself into a sitting position, the sheet pooling in his lap, and tugs Aidan the rest of the way in for a kiss.

Aidan's jacket is scratchy and *cold* against his skin, and he can't help but pull away.

"Sorry," Aidan says. "Let me change and we'll try that again."

"It's March," Kyle whines. "It shouldn't be this cold."

Aidan unzips his coat and drops it on the floor. He tosses his long-sleeve shirt in the laundry basket and pulls out an even softer shirt from his pajama drawer. "The radio says we're supposed to get snow tomorrow."

"Ugh." Just thinking about it makes Kyle want to put clothes on. "If it snows then we're spending the day cuddling on the couch. Hot chocolate is mandatory, TV is optional."

Aidan laughs as he switches his jeans out for flannel pajama pants. Kyle eyes the fabric and decides to make cuddling mandatory tonight too. Then Aidan yawns, his jaw cracking as it stretches too wide.

"Getting back in bed might not be the best idea," Kyle says.

"It's a great idea."

Kyle slides off the bed, the sheet still wrapped around his waist. "Too late." He scoops his shirt off the floor and puts it on before stealing a pair of Aidan's pajama pants. They're a little short on him, but he just takes a pair of socks to make up for it. "I read that you should stay up to eight, or later if possible."

"Did you look up tips to fight jet lag?"

"No." Kyle ducks his head, unsure why he's embarrassed. There's nothing wrong with wanting to make sure jet lag doesn't kick his partner's ass.

"Thank you. Eight might be a little ambitious, though." Aidan covers another yawn.

"We'll make dinner and you can tell me about your trip."

"We?"

"Cooking engages your hands and your head. It'll help keep you away."

"There are so many things I could say to that." Aidan crowds closer until he can wrap an arm around Kyle's waist. His fingers play with the hem of Kyle's shirt as if he's thinking about taking it off.

"If I thought we could have sex without you falling asleep then I would've stayed naked."

Aidan looks disappointed. "Tomorrow. Schedule it after the cuddling and the hot chocolate."

"Duly noted."

Aidan takes another step into Kyle's space until they're hip to hip. "I haven't said hello."

Kyle grins as he curls his fingers around Aidan's waist, holding him where he is. "Hi."

Aidan's eyes crinkle. "Can I kiss you?"

Kyle nods and closes his eyes. Anticipation grows as Aidan doesn't kiss him right away. His lips buzz, and his eyelids flutter, wanting to open and see if Aidan's any closer than he was before. But then Aidan's thighs press against his and a moment later, Kyle's finally being kissed. His entire body relaxes into Aidan's hold, moving even closer. It's been a long week apart.

Rather than making the kiss frantic, the reunion makes it sweet. There's no need to rush or even to cling, because he has Aidan back, and they have the entire night together and all of tomorrow. They could even have the day after if they want.

Kyle's chest is almost painful, as if there isn't enough space for all his feelings. His twines his fingers in the hem of Aidan's shirt and tugs as if having Aidan closer is the answer. Maybe if he shares some of what he's feeling, then it won't be so overwhelming.

Aidan sways into him, heavy, and almost knocks Kyle on his ass.

"Okay," Kyle says. "Food time. My ego can't handle it if you fall asleep on me."

Aidan's gaze is heavy lidded, and it would be alluring if he didn't look one breath away from not opening his eyes for the next ten hours. "First, a little nap."

Kyle gives him a push toward the door. "Food. And you're helping."

Aidan's pantry has a whole shelf dedicated to different kinds of pasta because boiling water and dumping pasta into it is about as advanced as his cooking gets. Kyle ignores the shelf, because Aidan just came home from Italy, and Kyle won't compete against that. He pulls out the box of white rice instead.

"This looks complicated," Aidan says. Then, after Kyle pulls a bag of frozen vegetables out of the freezer, "And healthy."

"Like us."

"We're complicated?" Aidan asks.

Well, Kyle's feelings are growing more complicated, but that doesn't mean the two of them are complicated. "Nah. Boy likes boy, that's as uncomplicated as it gets."

It's the right answer because Aidan smiles, soft and a little sleepy. He plucks the vegetables out of Kyle's hands and sets them on the counter before he goes up on his toes to kiss him. It's a lingering kiss but one without any intent behind it.

"I missed this," Aidan says as he pulls back.

"Kissing me?"

Aidan shrugs which isn't exactly an answer. "What're we doing with the rice and vegetables?"

Kyle grabs the eggs out of the fridge. "Can you guess now?"

Aidan shakes his head.

Kyle finds the sauce he wants in the pantry.

"Fried rice?" Aidan asks.

"Ding-ding-ding, we have a winner."

Aidan gives him a friendly shove and then, as if he can't stand Kyle to be so far away, immediately pulls him back to his side. They stay tucked together as Kyle starts dinner, using three of the four burners so he can cook the rice, the vegetables, and the eggs all at once.

"How?" Aidan asks as Kyle moves from pot to skillet to saucepan.

"Practice. You want to help?"

"I'm good."

Kyle pokes at the frozen block of vegetables, hoping to break it up a bit. "Next time we'll do this with fresh vegetables."

"Next time we make fried rice or next time I come home from Italy?"

They're close enough that it's obvious when Kyle draws up, pulling in on himself as if he can protect himself from an event that might not even happen. "You're going back?" *Will it be longer this time?*

It's stupid to think they'll never spend time apart, and it isn't healthy for them to be together all the time, but Kyle's just gotten Aidan back. He doesn't want to think about having to be apart from him again.

Aidan slips his hands up Kyle's shirt and draws him against his chest. "It's beautiful there. I wouldn't mind going back. Without students. I have a long winter break and an even longer summer break. We should see what your schedule looks like."

Kyle doesn't turn to look over his shoulder, because he's afraid of what his face will give away, but he does lean into Aidan's hold. Planning a vacation together is a big step, and one that makes him think offering Aidan a collar isn't such a far-fetched plan.

"I'm sure I can convince my boss to give me some time off," Kyle says.

"I don't know, I heard he's a stickler."

Now Kyle does turn, a happy smile stretched across his face. "I'll put in a good word for you."

They kiss, not as long as Kyle would like, because he's still making dinner. There'll be plenty of time to kiss later; today *and* even later than that. If Aidan's thinking toward the future then it means Kyle isn't the only one who wants more. It almost makes him wish this extension was over, if only so they can see whether they're on the same page.

Well, he supposes he could bring it up now, but a tiny bit of doubt makes him hold his tongue.

"Candles?" Kyle asks when they break apart.

"Is this a candle kind of dinner?"

"You've been gone for a week and now you're back so I'd say yeah."

Aidan squeezes Kyle's sides before he hunts down some candles. Because he only owns ones he's been gifted by students, he returns with Winter Wonderland and Log Cabin. They're not what Kyle would've picked for dinner, but it's the thought that counts, right?

They eat at the small table, sitting across from each other so they can tangle their feet under the table and gaze at each other over the flickering flames of the candles. Well, in theory, that's what dinner should be like. In reality, Kyle has to kick every time Aidan's eyes slip shut or his head dips down.

"There's no way I make it until eight," Aidan says.

It's 7:30. They could make a final push, but Aidan looks exhausted, and Kyle figures it's close enough.

"Help me with the dishes then we can go to bed."

"You don't have to come with me," Aidan says.

"I'll bring my phone and dim the backlight. I can read."

Aidan looks as if he's going to protest again.

"I want to be near you," Kyle says.

He makes sure to brush his teeth when Aidan does, and it's a good choice, because as soon as they're in bed, Aidan sprawls across him, a leg and an arm weighing Kyle down. Within minutes, Aidan's asleep, and Kyle doesn't want to move for fear of waking him up.

He reads a chapter in his book to make sure Aidan's well and truly asleep before he says, "I'm glad you're home."

Chapter Six

THE SENIOR ART Symposium is at the end of April. Kyle's been looking forward to it, both because he likes art and because he likes the idea of Aidan bringing him somewhere. They go to Enchanting Encounters together, and they'll meet up with Jenny and Charlotte for drinks sometimes, but going out with friends is different than being Aidan's plus-one. If they weren't spending the night surrounded by Aidan's students and his colleagues, then Kyle might be tempted to call it a date.

But they will be surrounded by Aidan's coworkers, he's essentially working after hours, so it *isn't* a date. It makes Kyle's nerves settle, because if it isn't a date, then he can't screw it up. It also makes him antsy, because he *wants* it to be a date.

He pulls a green crewneck sweatshirt over his head. It's Aidan's, the collar stretched out from multiple wears and the cuffs loose from being pushed up to his elbows. The college's name is printed across his chest in big white letters.

When he was in high school, he swiped his boyfriend's letterman jacket a few times, but the leather sleeves were stiff and it smelled musty like they stored the jackets in the storage room with all the football and hockey gear during the off-season.

Aidan's sweatshirt is much more comfortable. It smells better too, like coffee and detergent.

"Why are you smelling my sweatshirt?" Aidan asks. He rubs a towel through his hair then pauses as he says, "Why are you wearing my sweatshirt at all?"

"I'm supporting you," Kyle answers. Thankfully, winter appears to have given up, the snow from the latest storm finally melted away. It's warm enough now that he can wear a sweatshirt with a long-sleeve shirt underneath it and be fine. No more winter coat until next year.

"Supporting me," Aidan repeats.

"I can ditch the sweatshirt, but I have a college long-sleeve underneath it."

"When did you have time to raid my closet?"

Kyle looks pointedly at Aidan's towel. "You took too long in the shower."

"Ah, this is your revenge for taking separate showers. There's no way we'd make it on time if we showered together."

"Or we could've gotten ready earlier," Kyle says. He's disappointed with the lack of shower sharing and even more disappointed that Aidan changed in the bathroom.

"Brat," Aidan says.

Kyle tries not to light up too much as he asks, "Does that mean you'll spank me when we get home?"

Things have been hectic the past two weeks. Aidan's hurtling toward finals at an alarming speed which means endless papers to grade and extended office hours and students emailing him at all hours of the night. And Kyle's preparing for the Bondage Expo, which means he's trying to get ahead of his work so he won't have to worry about deadlines and clients while he's in Wisconsin.

They've been busy together, camping out at Kyle's island counter or spreading out on Aidan's living room floor, but it's been work. There hasn't been much time to play, and Kyle's antsy. It makes him act out and test the limits to see how far he can push before Aidan pushes back.

"A spanking isn't a deterrent when you want it this badly," Aidan says. He grabs a sweatshirt for himself and pulls it over his head. "And if you want something you can ask. I suppose I should be grateful you didn't wash all my towels again."

Kyle grins. In the beginning, Aidan never took his clothes off when Kyle could see him. He claims it wasn't a thing, but it was totally a thing. When Kyle grew tired of it, he washed all the towels in Aidan's apartment while he was in the shower. It ended with Kyle being tied up and able to look at Aidan but not allowed to touch.

It was worth it.

But Kyle isn't looking for a punishment tonight.

He slinks up to Aidan and fusses with his sweatshirt, an excuse to stand close. "This is me asking," he says.

Aidan's eyes crinkle as he smiles. "I'll give you a chance to ask me nicer when we come home."

Kyle leans in for a kiss, a brief brush of lips. He pulls back before he's tempted to try for more. He's actually looking forward to tonight, and he doesn't want to be late. He clasps Aidan's hands and tugs him toward the door.

"Does your school have a fight song or something?"

"It's an art show, not the Homecoming football game," Aidan says.

"That's totally a yes. You're teaching me in the car."

"I am, am I?"

"There are soccer games in our future," Kyle answers. "I need to make sure I'm ready."

"You want to watch the women's soccer team?"

"Caroline coaches them. It's obviously something important to her and she's our friend, so…" Kyle shrugs as if this isn't a big deal. Though, maybe he should've said *she's your friend*. Caroline and Ritchie are Aidan's friends the way Jenny and Charlotte are Kyle's. Is he blending their lives too quickly? He's never been good a space, or moderation.

Aidan squeezes his hand, pulling Kyle out of his downward spiral. "I bet you're good at face paint."

"I can paint a mean butterfly. Learning to do a falcon might take some practice."

"I guess we'll have to see a bunch of games then."

Kyle grins and bumps his shoulder against Aidan's.

THE PERFORMING AND visual arts have an entire building dedicated to them. It's a modern building, all glass and sleek lines. On the lawn in front of it are sculptures and art installations. Kyle stops by a bench with a statue of a woman knitting.

"Unique."

"Every school has to have something. The kids take selfies with it. Extra points if they're knitting in their picture."

"We had this water feature that was a long slanted slab of marble."

"Oh no."

Kyle laughs. "Oh yes. There was a lot of naked slip-and-sliding."

He eyes the statue, her arms raised as she knits what looks like the beginning of a scarf. He drops down onto the bench next to her and pats his lap.

"No," Aidan says, but he's smiling. It means he's open to being convinced.

"It's a tradition," Kyle says. He tugs on his sweatshirt, showing off the school's name. "Come on. Show your pride."

There are a couple of people headed into the building and even more roaming the sidewalks that crisscross, connecting the art building to the student center and to the main walkway leading down to the library and the science labs. Aidan's promised him a full tour another time.

Now, Kyle holds up his phone and Aidan huffs but sits down next to him on the bench. It's a tight squeeze, the two of them and the statue.

"You're on the outside," Kyle says, handing Aidan his phone.

He pulls Aidan closer to him and smiles even though the statue's elbow digs into his back. Aidan takes their selfie and then shakes his head as Kyle immediately sets it as his background picture. It isn't a great angle and Aidan's arm takes up a third of the shot, but it's the two of them—and Knitting Lady—so he keeps it.

They're greeted at the doors by a student handing out paper programs listing each project and who created it.

"Hi, professor," the girl says as she hands him a program. She glances at Kyle, clearly curious. "Hi, professor's friend. Do you need a program too?"

"Nah, we'll share," Kyle says. "Do you have anything on display tonight?"

"I'm only a junior."

"She's not part of the senior exhibit, but Margot was the photographer for our production of *Twelfth Night*. Her work's outside the stage."

Margot ducks her head as she scuffs one of her Converse on the floor.

"My friend makes her living off being a photographer," Kyle says and Margot glances up at him. "I don't have the patience for it, but she can happily adjust the lighting on a shoot for half an hour."

"Lighting's important." Margot takes a deep breath as if she's about to launch into a passionate defense of light sources and the importance of shadows. But then she snaps her mouth shut and looks at the floor again.

Kyle knows that look. He's had too many people zone out while he's talked about how choosing the wrong font can completely derail a project to misunderstand Margot's sudden shyness. She's holding herself back and he figures she's had too many people cut her off or put her down while she talks about what she loves.

"Are you stuck on door duty all night?" Kyle asks.

"Just the first shift."

"Find us later. I want to see your photographs. It isn't fair that the seniors get all the attention tonight."

"I mean, it is fair," she says. "Tonight is all about them. But if you have time later, then I can show you some stuff. The costuming department did a really good job."

They're holding up the line so they have to move along, but Kyle makes a mental note to find her later. Inside the doors, they can go left or right. The large sign points them left so, naturally, Kyle tries to go right.

"That's toward the stage," Aidan says. "We'll go that way later."

They fall into step behind a group of students and follow them into a big open room. Paintings and photographs hang on the walls and 3-D designs hang from the ceiling and sculptures and installations are set up on the floor.

Kyle's drawn to the big piece in the middle. It's shards of dishware which have been fused together until they're shaped like a heart.

"*The Anatomy of a Breakup*," Kyle reads. "Huh. This doesn't look fun. Luckily, I've missed it."

"Breakups?"

"Having dishes thrown at my head." He circles around the installation and winces at the sheer number of plates making up the piece. Hopefully they all weren't thrown at the artist. "It seems like it would hurt."

"It did," says the kid who's hovering by the installation. His jeans are ripped at the knees, but he's wearing a dress shirt and a tie as if he remembered at the last minute that he was supposed to look nice for the presentation. "Luckily, I got my arms up, so I didn't take any of the plates to the face."

"You should work on those amicable breakups," Kyle tells him. "This is cool, though." He catches Aidan watching him and raises his eyebrows. "You seriously thought I've never been dumped?"

"I figured you were the one who ended things."

Hardly. Kyle's the one who clings. He's the one who tries to make things work for a few miserable weeks before he's forced to admit things aren't working. Lately, he's avoided breakups all together by only hooking up with people at Enchanting Encounters. They set specific timetables for their relationship and when it ends, they both go their separate ways. There are people he cycles back to, Renee's one of his favorite scene partners, but they've never had the kind of relationship where either of them would break up with the other.

Aidan's the first person Kyle's been in both a romantic and sexual relationship with in a long time. And there's no way Kyle will be the one to end things. He wants Aidan for as long as Aidan will have him. But even if that turns out to be after this extension, he can't see them ending in shattered dishes.

Shattered feelings, but not ceramics.

The kid's watching the two of them a little too closely so Kyle forces himself to shrug, casual. "Not usually. Is this piece part of a large collection?"

"I have something in every room," the kid answers. "If you pass through the gallery counterclockwise, then you'll see the relationship backward."

"Cool."

They move to the far wall where more traditional paintings hang. They're a series of still lifes, but as Kyle gets closer, he realizes they each have a twist. The orange in the fruit bowl is growing mold and the pair of scissors in the open drawer reflect a woman crying. From a distance, the paintings look like something in a beginner's textbook but up close they're so much more.

"Your kids are clever," Kyle says.

"Most of them aren't mine. If they're an art major, then they're required to take a certain number of art history courses, but it's not their focus."

"Don't let Prof sell himself short," a young woman says. Her shawl drapes over her shoulders like a melting clock.

"Very Dali," Kyle tells her.

She beams. Thank you. Professor A's the one who convinced me to give art a try. He told me if I worked hard enough then one day he'd give lectures on *my* work."

"These are yours then?"

She nods and holds her hand out. "Emmalee Grant."

"I'm Kyle," he says as he shakes her hand. "I like the approach. I always found beginner art classes boring, but this is a way to spice them up."

"You're an artist too? Is that how you and Professor A met?"

"We met through a friend," Kyle says and winces. That's as close as he can get to confirming they're together without kissing Aidan in the middle of the room. Aidan's colleagues know Aidan and Kyle are together—at least, Ritchie does—but Kyle isn't sure if that's something Aidan wants his students to know. He doesn't even know if Aidan's out to his students.

"Kyle's a graphic designer," Aidan answers. He curls a hand around Kyle's hip which is a yes on letting people know they're together. "He's also putting a modern twist on traditional art."

"Flatterer," Kyle says.

"I'm just speaking the truth," Aidan says and he winks at Emmalee.

Kyle elbows him as Emmalee laughs.

"Laura's set up in the next room. She's made an homage to Eleanor."

"Eleanor?" Kyle asks.

"Our knitter," Emmalee answers. "She's outside on the bench."

"We took a selfie with her on our way in. Aidan says it's a tradition."

"One of our best." Emmalee glances between them before she smiles. "I hope you enjoy the rest of your night. There's supposedly a table with crackers and cheese and fruit somewhere."

"We'll leave the free food for the college kids," Kyle says. "You probably need it more than we do."

THEY CYCLE THROUGH the rooms until they've seen all the displays. They're studying a collection of campaign buttons when Aidan nudges him and tilts his head to the right. Kyle glances that way and spots Margot hovering by the torn movie tickets marking the beginning of the relationship that ended in shattered plates.

"One last stop?" Kyle asks.

"We don't have to."

"I promised her," Kyle says. "Besides, when I was her age, it meant a lot to me whenever someone cared. Self-motivation has never been one of my strengths. It's why I freelance. People come to me wanting my work. It's what gives me the push I need to create."

Aidan smiles at him, fond and soft and something else that makes Kyle's chest clench. He smiles and leans into Aidan's side before approaching Margot.

IT'S NEARING ELEVEN when they get home. Kyle covers a yawn as he kicks his shoes off by the door. Aidan bends down to untie his, but that's as much effort as he puts in. He still slides them off, leaving them in a heap next to Kyle's.

"Who thought a late-night art showing on a Monday night was a good idea?" Kyle asks.

"Tired?"

"Little bit but I'm not the one who has to teach tomorrow."

"Not until the afternoon." Aidan hangs his coat up. He holds his hand out for Kyle's before he seems to remember Kyle didn't wear a coat. "I still can't believe you wore my sweatshirt."

Kyle leans against the closed door and offers up his sleaziest smile. "Is that your way of saying you want me to take it off?"

"I thought it was late and you're too tired?"

Kyle pushes off the door and hooks his fingers through Aidan's belt loops. "You promised you'd spank me."

"I don't think that's how the conversation went."

"Please?" Kyle asks. He tugs Aidan closer to him until they're thigh to thigh. "You said it yourself, you don't have classes until the afternoon. We can stay up late then sleep in."

Aidan tries hard to look stern, but he can't keep the smile off his face. "I guess we don't have to sleep yet. Bedroom. I want your clothes off and your cuffs waiting for me when I get there."

He swats Kyle on the ass, a preview of what's to come, and Kyle grins as he saunters down the hall. This is exactly what he's needed; Aidan looming over him and holding him down. It's not that having dinner together is bad or working side by side is boring, but he's missed the way Aidan's hand closes around his wrists as if he needs Kyle so badly he has to hold him down to make sure he stays.

As soon as he's in Aidan's room, he strips out of his clothes and tosses them in Aidan's full laundry basket. He'll run a load in the morning. As a reward, he'll swipe one of Aidan's shirts out of the dryer to bring home with him.

He takes his cuffs out of his bag and lays them on the edge of the bed before he kneels. The bedroom door is to his left, just out of his line of vision, but he hears Aidan's footsteps as he approaches the room.

There's a pause as he stops. Kyle imagines Aidan standing in the doorway, caught off guard by Kyle kneeling here even though he's the one who told him to do it. He's tempted to turn his head and see if Aidan's watching him, but he doesn't need to. He can feel the weight of Aidan's gaze as it trails down his back.

He shudders, breathing out on a shaky exhale. Aidan's gaze almost feels like a touch, solid enough that he wants to press back into it but light enough that he shivers. He wants Aidan's hands to skim down the same path. He wants one of Aidan's hands, firm, on the back of his neck as he guides Kyle into position.

"I don't think I could ever get tired of this," Aidan says.

Me either.

He can see Aidan approach out of the corner of his eye, but he doesn't turn until Aidan threads his fingers through Kyle's hair and turns his head for him. With Kyle on his knees, Aidan's finally taller, and Kyle's able to look up at him through his lashes. Often it's a move he uses to start something. But he doesn't need to do that tonight. They've agreed to a plan, which means he's lost some of his earlier, restless energy.

He can be patient as he looks up at Aidan from the floor.

Aidan brushes his thumb across Kyle's bottom lip. "You look beautiful here like this."

Kyle holds his wrists out, an offering.

"Is this what you want?"

"Yeah," Kyle answers.

Aidan buckles Kyle's cuffs on and then, still holding his wrists, sits down on the edge of the bed. "I want you over my lap."

He reluctantly drops Kyle's wrists so Kyle can stand and arrange himself over Aidan's lap. He feels too big like this. It probably looks weird from the outside, but there's no one here to watch them. There's only the two of them.

"You aren't allowed to come from this, no matter how good it feels."

Aidan squeezes the back of Kyle's neck with one hand. The other rests on the small of Kyle's back. Like this, held between Aidan's legs and his hands, he feels surrounded and protected in the best of ways.

He sinks deeper into Aidan's hold and into his own thoughts.

"Please," Kyle asks as his feelings threaten to rise up and overwhelm him. The things he wants are too much. He needs Aidan to knock it all out of his head. He wants his world to narrow down to the sting of his skin and the rhythm of Aidan's hand.

"I love it when you ask me to hurt you."

Even though Kyle knows it's coming, the first blow catches him off guard. He gasps and then tenses up, shock more than pain. Aidan's free hand squeezes his neck again, reassuring. Once Kyle relaxes, Aidan hits him again.

It takes five blows for his body to go limp in Aidan's hold. He doesn't anticipate the hits and doesn't try to brace for them. He exhales and his muscles lose the last of their remaining tension as he gives himself over to Aidan's care.

Aidan spanks him faster after that, never hitting him in the same place twice in a row. There's no set pattern for Kyle to follow. Even as he sinks deeper into his head, Aidan doesn't let him slip completely under. He's here and present, aware of every sting and slap and the hot burn of his skin.

Aidan scratches his fingers lightly through Kyle's hair, offering comfort with one hand while giving Kyle pain with the other. Kyle pings from one sensation to the other, arching into the scalp massage and then pressing into the hard slap of Aidan's palm.

They're both good, and he doesn't have to choose between them, because Aidan offers both, and he decides when to give them. Two sharp cracks of his hand and he runs his fingers through Kyle's hair until he's limp over Aidan's lap. Then the hardest hit yet, one that makes Kyle cry out, the noise somewhere between hurt and needy.

When Aidan finally stops, they're both breathing heavily.

Aidan's hand rests just above the swell of Kyle's ass, where his skin is red. He wriggles a bit, trying to get Aidan's hand lower. He wants Aidan to hit him again, but he's afraid he won't be able to hold himself in check. His cock is hard and leaking against Aidan's pants. It would be easy to rut against Aidan's thigh until he comes, but Aidan told him not to.

He focuses on the pleasant buzz under his skin instead of the throb of his erection. He feels good, floating and grounded at the same time. He wants Aidan to feel as good as he's made Kyle feel.

He slides to his knees. Aidan tries to hold on to him, but his body feels more liquid than solid, and he slips through Aidan's grasp.

He nudges Aidan's knees apart, making a space for himself. There's a wet spot on Aidan's pants and Kyle breathes hot over it, making it wetter. Then he licks it, the denim rough under his tongue. He slides his hands up Aidan's thighs, but Aidan catches him there, holds him down.

He eyes Aidan's zipper. "Please? You gave me what I wanted. Let me do the same."

"I want to see my handiwork," Aidan says. "Lie down on the bed, on your stomach."

As soon as Aidan releases him, he moves, stretching out across the bed. The comforter is cool against his overheated skin. His dick ends up trapped between his stomach and the bed which is just uncomfortable enough to feel good.

Aidan straddles his thighs, jeans scraping against Kyle's skin. He shivers and presses his legs firmly against Aidan's, needing to be touched.

"I did good with you tonight," Aidan says.

He palms Kyle's ass, sliding his hands down the reddened skin and back up. Kyle hums, pleased with the praise even though he didn't have much to do with it. Aidan touches him as if he's trying to commit the moment to memory, as if Kyle wouldn't let him do this any time Aidan asked.

"I want to come on you," Aidan says.

"Yes." Kyle twists to look over his shoulder.

Aidan kisses him, gentle, and then guides Kyle's head back to the bed. "Stay."

"I want to see."

"Not tonight." Aidan leans down to kiss him again, an apology.

Kyle closes his eyes because it's the best way to avoid temptation. He's rewarded with another kiss. This one is lingering as if Aidan doesn't want to pull away. Eventually, he does, and Kyle's body aches to follow him, but he stays where he's been put. He trusts that whatever Aidan's about to do will be just as good.

Of course, that's when Aidan pulls back completely. The bed dips as Aidan slides off it. Kyle wants to open his eyes and flip over, he wants to make sure Aidan isn't leaving him. He made all these promises, told Kyle he'd been good and this is his reward? Being left alone?

Aidan wraps his fingers around Kyle's ankle, a reassurance that he's still here.

"Cross your wrists behind your back," Aidan says.

He does, his wrists resting against the small of his back. He curls his fingers so they only just brush the swell of his ass. Aidan trails his fingertips down the inside of Kyle's forearms, from his elbows to his cuffs to his palms. Kyle reaches for Aidan's fingers and they hold hands for two breaths before Aidan's touch disappears.

"I'm undressing," Aidan says.

Kyle whines, unhappy that he's being denied the sight of it.

"I'm going to kneel astride your thighs and paint your ass with my come and that isn't enough for you?"

"I want everything," Kyle says. "You know that."

"I do." His voice is warm again, approving, and Kyle's chest aches with how good it sounds.

"Thank you for making a mess of me."

"I haven't done it yet."

"But you will. You said you would, and you keep your promises."

Aidan squeezes Kyle's ankle again. "Sometimes, I think I'm the one being spoiled. You're so good for me."

"You make it easy."

Aidan kisses him again, slow and thorough, until Kyle's back twinges from twisting to meet him. They keep kissing after that, desperate, as if they're both chasing something. *I'm right here*, Kyle wants to say. *You don't have to worry.*

When Aidan breaks the kiss, Kyle opens his eyes. Aidan's eyes are open too, staring. There's the barest hint of stubble coming in on Aidan's chin. He'll probably shave tomorrow morning. Aidan's always been clean-shaven, his face smooth. Kyle wonders what it would feel like to him to leave beard burn behind.

Aidan pulls back and Kyle settles against the bed again without being asked. He crosses his wrists the way they were before. Aidan drops a kiss between his shoulder blades.

Kyle hears the click of the lube cap opening. His ears strain for more sounds; the exhale when Aidan first touches himself, the squelch of lube, Aidan's soft groan.

Kyle closes his eyes. He tries to imagine what Aidan sees. Kyle laid out on the bed exactly as Aidan's asked, his eyes closed and wrists crossed because he knows how to listen. His reddened ass, proof of what they'd done earlier tonight.

Aidan curls his fingers around Kyle's wrist, their only point of contact. His breathing comes quicker and he squeezes Kyle's wrists, signs that he's getting closer. When he comes, he stripes Kyle's ass and the tops of his thighs with it.

Kyle finally feels *settled*. He turns his head to smile contentedly over his shoulder. "Thank you."

"Thank *you*." Aidan stretches out on the bed next to him so that Kyle doesn't have to crane his neck. He uses sticky fingers to rub circles against Kyle's back. "I should get a washcloth."

"In a few minutes."

They linger there until Aidan levers himself out of bed. He returns in pajama pants and a white T-shirt with a washcloth in his hand. He's gentle as he wipes the come off Kyle's skin. He tosses it into the laundry basket. Kyle should definitely do laundry in the morning.

"What're you thinking about?" Aidan asks as he pulls the covers back as best he can with Kyle stretched out across them.

"Laundry."

Aidan stares at him for a long moment before he bursts into surprised laughter. "Laundry? Should I be insulted?"

"Nah." Kyle rolls onto his side so Aidan can pull the covers back even more. He props himself up on his elbow. He can't help his glance at his cock, still hard, but not nearly as insistent as earlier.

"Will you wait until tomorrow morning?" Aidan asks.

Kyle's cuffs are still on, but he knows it's an honest question. If he says yes, Aidan will let him come. If he doesn't...well, half the fun is seeing what Aidan's plan is.

"Why?" Kyle asks.

"I want you to wake up desperate for me."

It's honest and Aidan ducks his head like he's ashamed of it. Kyle doesn't want that. He tugs Aidan closer until they're lying side by side, their faces only a few inches apart.

"I'll wait," Kyle says. "I might wake you up early, though."

"It'll be worth it."

Kyle draws Aidan in for a kiss, curling his hand around Aidan's neck and holding him close. His eyes are heavy, and sleep pulls him down, but he doesn't want to stop kissing Aidan. He knows Aidan will be here in the morning, they both will, but he still feels as if he needs to hoard every moment they have together.

He wonders if he'll ever stop feeling this way, like what he has isn't enough or like he might lose it without warning.

Aidan runs his fingers over the buckles on Kyle's cuffs and Kyle shakes his head, careful so he doesn't break the kiss. Aidan rolls onto his back and pulls Kyle on top of him.

His cuffs stay on.

Chapter Seven

THERE ARE A few things on Kyle's fantasy checklist that he wants to do before the school year ends and Aidan's on summer break. For this one, he spends the day at the house while Aidan's teaching. It's difficult to concentrate, because his gaze is constantly drawn to the clock, and he wishes time would tick by faster.

Making dinner is a good way to pass an hour, but he hasn't made any progress on his to-do list for work when he hears a car door shut.

He saves the graphic he was half-heartedly working on and then shuts his computer.

He's spent the whole day thinking about how to start the evening. Would he pull Aidan in for a kiss first? Would they make it to the couch or could Kyle hold out long enough to make it to the bedroom? With the impatience that has been building all day, they'll be lucky if Kyle manages to shut the front door before pouncing.

Kyle checks the lock on the adjoining door to make sure Ritchie won't interrupt them. He's been better about knocking now he knows Kyle and Aidan are together, but it's still safer to lock the door. He's run through his plans for the night since he woke up this morning, and he doesn't want anything to mess with them.

Aidan pushes the door open with his hip. He has a messenger bag slung over his shoulder, a stack of folders in one hand, and his lunch box in the other. His hair is sticking up in every direction as if he ran his hands through it while grading papers.

He pauses when he sees Kyle clearly waiting for him. "Is everything all right?"

"It's good," Kyle promises. He slinks forward, taking the files from Aidan's grip and setting them on the couch. He drops his lunch box there too then holds his hand out for Aidan's bag.

"Are you sure?" Aidan asks as he hands it over. He nudges the door shut with his foot.

Kyle drops the bag on the couch, trusting the cushions to protect Aidan's laptop. Then he crowds Aidan against the door and drops his knees. "Welcome home."

"Uh." Aidan stares down at him, mouth parted around words he doesn't have the breath to say.

Kyle rubs his cheek against the front of Aidan's pants. Before he closes his eyes or sinks too deeply into what he wants, he forces himself to look up. "Is this okay?"

Aidan nods. He still looks dazed, words escaping him. Satisfaction blossoms in Kyle's chest, because he's the one to make Aidan look like this, eyes wide and cheeks flushed. He wants to see how long he can draw it out for.

"I've been thinking about this all day." Kyle pops the button on Aidan's pants. "I wanted to surprise you when you came home." He drags the zipper down as slowly as he can manage. "You're always taking care of me, and I wanted to return the favor. A blowjob when you walked through the door, dinner, something after."

"That's quite the hello," Aidan says, his voice soft, almost disbelieving.

Kyle tugs his pants down to his knees, giving him room to work. Aidan isn't completely hard yet, but the bulge of his cock still presses against the flimsy white fabric of his boxer briefs. Kyle glances up at Aidan, aware of how eager he looks and proud of it.

"Can I?"

Aidan smiles and drops a hand to Kyle's hair, his grip firm but not painful. He seems to have gotten over his initial shock and is onboard with Kyle's plans for the night. Kyle shamelessly dips his gaze down to Aidan's dick and wets his lips. Aidan has a tendency to draw things out until Kyle's desperate, but he's already spent the entire day waiting for this.

"Please?" Kyle asks.

"Like this." Aidan adjusts himself until his cock curves up, the head almost poking out of his waistband.

Kyle wants Aidan to tug his briefs down, even if it's only enough to expose the tip of his cock. Instead, he pushes Kyle's head down until he can mouth at his balls and up the hardening shaft of his cock. The fabric grows damp under his attention as he works his way up and then back down again.

He tries to fit his mouth around Aidan's cock, but as he moves up to the head, the fabric pulls too tight for him to even get the tip. He huffs out an annoyed breath and hooks his fingers in the elastic band so he can pull them down himself.

"No," Aidan says. He ruffles Kyle's hair to take the sting out of the word. "If you're that desperate then you can just use your mouth."

He looks up, his cheek resting against the hard line of Aidan's cock. His fingers are still curled around the waistband. He blinks through the haze of *want* and *need* and *now* as he tries to focus on what Aidan said.

Aidan's patient with him, running his hands through his hair and watching until the words sink in. Kyle drops his hands to his thighs, palms flat against his pants to avoid temptation. When Aidan doesn't say anything, he moves again. He clasps his hands behind his back, his right hand wrapped firmly around his left wrist.

The position leaves him balanced on his knees. It's even easier to stay the way he is, his face pressed against Aidan's cock, so close to what he wants. But he wants more than the hot feel of it through Aidan's briefs. He wants skin against skin, to feel and then taste.

Does no hands mean Kyle has to use his teeth? He's tried it enough to know that's too awkward to be sexy. He can't help his whine, frustrated, because he had plans for tonight, and Aidan's throwing up roadblocks. He knows exactly what he wants, but he doesn't know how to get it.

He—oh.

Aidan said to *use his mouth*.

Kyle's gaze flicks upward again.

Aidan watches him, a smile curving his lips.

"Help me?"

"Help you with what?"

Even though he's the one who planned the scene, Kyle still flushes when he realizes he'll have to spell it out. He should've known that even when trying to do something nice for Aidan, he would make him work for it. He shifts his weight from one knee to the other, liking the thought more than he should.

Aidan smiles as if he knows what Kyle's thinking. He probably does. They've been together long enough to know each other's buttons. Kyle is enthusiastic about sex, and even more enthusiastic about pleasing his partners, and the way Aidan takes that desire and twists it just enough to make him flush winds him up every time.

"Take off your briefs," Kyle asks. "I want to get my mouth on your cock. I want to show you what I've been thinking about all day."

Aidan tightens his hold in Kyle's hair, a warning to hold still and against taking anything he isn't given. Then he tugs down the left side of his briefs. If it had been the right side, then the head of his cock would be free. Instead, Aidan reveals a hipbone.

"May I?" Kyle asks.

After a nod, he leans in to press a kiss against the smooth patch of skin. He runs his tongue over the bump of Aidan's hipbone and kisses the wet spot he left behind. He presses a kiss to each knuckle of Aidan's hand, a thank-you, before he looks up again.

"More?"

Trapped between Kyle and the door, Aidan's careful as he takes his shoes and then his pants and briefs off. He's left in just his dress shirt, and it's long enough to cover his cock, hiding himself from Kyle's view once again.

"Really?" Kyle can't quite help how unimpressed he sounds.

Aidan just laughs and pushes his shirt up. He wraps his hand around his cock and strokes it to full hardness. "Is this what you want?" There's a taunting lilt to the words. Aidan knows it's what Kyle wants. But he also likes to wind him up, better at it than anyone Kyle's ever been with.

"*Please.*"

Aidan's expression softens. "Open."

Kyle parts his lips and holds still as Aidan drags the head of his cock across his top lip then the bottom one. He resists the urge to chase the smear of precome left behind.

He keeps his gaze raised, lets Aidan see every bit of impatience and every wave of want.

He's rewarded when Aidan finally slides his cock into Kyle's mouth. His tongue flutters, but he holds still and breathes carefully through his nose. He doesn't want to do something wrong and lose what little he's been given, but it's a struggle not to move.

This is what he's wanted since he woke up this morning, and he's finally on the cusp of having it.

"I've given you what you want." Aidan cards his hands through Kyle's hair. "Show me you're grateful."

It's the permission Kyle needs to surge forward and *take*. After being denied, he takes too much too fast, and he pulls off, gasping for breath. His eyes sting with tears, but he dives back in. Aidan tangles his fingers in Kyle's hair, but he doesn't pull him off or try to dictate his pace.

He thanks Aidan by paying attention to every inch of Aidan's cock, first with his lips and his tongue and then, gently, with his teeth. Aidan groans as Kyle's teeth scrape his sensitive flesh, and his hands tighten in Kyle's hair, but he doesn't pull him off.

"You've gotten good at this," Aidan says. He's leaning against the door now, depending on it to help him stay on his feet, and Kyle takes it as a compliment.

He knew how to give a blowjob before Aidan, but their months together have made him better at knowing what Aidan likes. He knows when to take it slow, teasing them both until one of them snaps. He knows when Aidan wants him passive, letting Aidan dictate the pace, and when he's allowed to take what he wants.

Tonight, he preens under the praise and takes just the tip of Aidan's cock into his mouth. He lets it poke the inside of his cheek, and Aidan traces his fingers over the bulge. His touch is featherlight as if he can't believe what he's seeing.

When Aidan's hand drops away, Kyle pulls off to nuzzle his cock until spit and precome are smeared across both his cheeks. He wants to feel owned by the end of the night. He wants Aidan on him, *in* him, wants to be surrounded by the man until his entire world narrows down to the two of them.

This time, when he takes Aidan deep, he's prepared for it. He doesn't choke, doesn't have to pull back and cough. He slides forward until his nose presses against the coarse hair scattered across Aidan's skin. He's tempted to shut his eyes and *bask*, but he leaves them open. The scent of sex is heady this close, and he can taste it in the back of his throat. Everything is Aidan, what he sees and touches and smells, and it's almost perfect. He just needs—

"You're so good at this," Aidan says.

Kyle's eyes flutter shut for a moment and he tries to press even closer. "I should have you welcome me home like this every day."

He would if Aidan wanted him to. For variety's sake, he'd make sure to switch it up. A drawn out hand job one day, something quick and dirty on the next. He quirks his lips up in a smile, hoping it shows he's on board with this plan.

"You like that idea?" Aidan laughs and tugs on Kyle's hair. He moans around the cock in his mouth and Aidan's head thunks against the door. "Of course you do. I would send you a text before I left work, telling you how I wanted to find you when I came through the door, and you'd listen, wouldn't you?"

Kyle nods.

"You always listen."

Kyle pulls back to draw in a deep breath. He licks down Aidan's cock, gentle when he reaches his balls. They're full and heavy, warm against his tongue. He sucks one into his mouth and hums.

Aidan tightens his grip, pulling at Kyle's hair until it stings. It's the perfect kind of pain, and he moans this time.

"I want to come in your mouth," Aidan says. "Will you let me?"

It's a warning as much as it is a question. Kyle abandons his teasing to take Aidan in his mouth again. He bobs his head, hard suction followed by soothing strokes of his tongue. Aidan's hands tug harder on his hair as he gets closer. His breathing picks up too, short choppy gasps that Kyle drinks up. He loves the sting in his scalp and the tremble in Aidan's legs and the loud sound of his breathing, all the little signs that point to him being able to affect Aidan as much as Aidan affects him.

When he comes, Kyle swallows then pulls away before Aidan can push him off. He lets go of his wrist and shakes his arms out as he stands.

"I'm going to put dinner in the oven," Kyle says. He brushes a kiss across Aidan's cheek and leaves him leaning half-naked against the door.

He sets the oven to 350 then puts the tinfoil covered dish inside. When he turns back around, he has a clear view of the living room. Aidan's pulled his boxer briefs back on, but he's left his pants in a pile on the floor.

"No-pants dinner?" Kyle asks. His voice is gravelly, and he rubs his throat even though it won't do anything to help.

Aidan's gaze darkens for a moment, possessive and wanting. Kyle drops his hand to his side and wonders if their after-dinner activities will have a rougher edge. He wouldn't mind being held down and *fucked*, Aidan pressing his face into the mattress as he takes what he wants.

"Less work to do later," Aidan says. He crowds Kyle against the island counter, pulling him from thoughts of later back into the present. "But it means you're overdressed."

"Smooth."

Kyle laughs as Aidan undoes the button on his pants. Aidan grins as he eases the zipper down.

"After dinner, it's your show," Aidan says. "Anything you want, tell me, and I'll give it to you."

He sinks gracefully to his knees as he tugs Kyle's pants off. He glances up and grins at the stunned expression on Kyle's face. Is this what he wants? Aidan blows him sometimes, usually only after he's told Kyle he can't come because he's a particular kind of sadist, but if Kyle asked, he wouldn't tease tonight.

Anything he wants is an overwhelming offer. And a little bit unfair. Back when they first started, Kyle offered Aidan anything, and Aidan almost safe worded out of the scene. He cautioned Kyle against making such an open-ended offer, and now he's offering the same thing? Because he trusts Kyle more than he trusts himself? Because they both know that *anything* is still contained by hard nos and softer maybes?

"You don't have to decide now," Aidan says.

He leaves Kyle's pants in a pile on the floor then stands so they can kiss. He has to tilt his head up to reach, and Kyle meets his mouth eagerly. He palms Aidan's ass as they kiss, careful not to rub up against him. It's too soon after he's come to feel good and even though Kyle likes that kind of overstimulation, he knows Aidan didn't.

Then, as Aidan snaps the waistband of Kyle's briefs, he remembers that he hasn't set a timer.

He breaks the kiss with a regretful, "Just a second." He jabs at the buttons on the oven until thirty minutes pop up. He won't ruin a good night by burning dinner.

When he turns back around, Aidan's sitting on the counter, his legs spread so Kyle has a place to stand.

"You just like being tall," Kyle accuses.

Aidan laughs and doesn't deny it.

THEY EAT DINNER at the island, neither of them wearing pants, and their lips puffy from kissing for so long. If the timer hadn't gone off, then Kyle would've been happy to keep kissing. Maybe that's what he'll ask for tonight, for the two of them to trade lazy kisses until he falls asleep.

Part of him thinks he should have a more exciting answer to *anything you want*, but he doesn't. He wants something slow and sweet. Earlier, he thought he wanted something with an edge, but he's changed his mind.

They're doing the dishes when Kyle says, "I want you to fuck me." He scrunches up his nose because that isn't the right word. "Slowly. I want you to spread me out on your bed and take your time."

Aidan sets the plates on the drying rack. "Anything else?"

"You can decide the rest."

Aidan looks like he's going to push for more of an answer before he holds his hand out to Kyle. They head into the bedroom together, and Kyle stops by his bag to pull his cuffs out. He didn't wear them earlier, but now he wants the steady press of the leather against his skin so it'll feel as if Aidan's holding him even when his hands are elsewhere.

He holds them out in offering.

"Clothes off first then I'll put them on for you."

He sets his cuffs on the bed and pulls his T-shirt over his head. It lands in the laundry basket. His briefs miss by a couple feet.

"A for effort," Aidan tells him.

"Shame, I was hoping for the D."

Aidan pauses, his shirt unbuttoned and hanging off his arms. He stares, mouth working soundlessly for a moment, before he finally says, "I can't believe you."

Kyle grins as he drops down on to the bed. "You gave me the opening. Speaking of openings..."

"I'm going to gag you," Aidan threatens. "You're full of terrible lines tonight."

Kyle waggles his eyebrows. He has a few ideas of what he's hoping to be full of soon, but Aidan covers his mouth with his hand before he can say any of them. Kyle grins and then licks Aidan's palm.

"Brat," Aidan says fondly. "Give me your wrists."

He holds them out and keeps his mouth shut as Aidan buckles them on. He takes his time even though they've done this enough that he could probably do it with his eyes closed. When the second one is secured around his wrist, something in Kyle settles.

"Thank you."

Aidan tips his chin up and kisses him. It's sweet, lingering as if Aidan doesn't want to stop. He pulls away only to lean back in for another kiss. Kyle sinks deeper and deeper into the mattress until he wants to forget about the sex and just do this for the rest of the night. He wraps his arms around Aidan's neck to hold him here which is, of course, when Aidan pulls away for real.

"How do you want it?" Aidan asks.

"Like this." On his back so he can see Aidan's face. Kyle spreads his legs, an encouragement and invitation in one. "Please?"

"Shh." Aidan gently closes Kyle's mouth. "You don't have to beg. Anything you want tonight, I'll give it to you."

Again, that open-ended promise. He's starting to understand why Aidan flinched away from it when Kyle offered. It's so much. *Anything.*

"Will you take your clothes off?" Kyle asks. "All of them?"

Aidan smiles and slides off the bed. He tosses his button-up over his dresser and then throws his undershirt and briefs in the laundry basket. Kyle stays where he is, stretched out across the bed as Aidan pulls the lube out of the bedside drawer. He holds up a condom in question.

Kyle shakes his head. "I want to feel you."

Aidan puts the condom back and kneels between Kyle's legs. He squeezes a bit of lube onto his fingers then warms it up.

"You're going to spoil me." Kyle lifts his knees to his chest to make it easier for Aidan to prep him.

"Says the one who greeted me with a blowjob and dinner."

"That was just foreplay. If you're worried, though, I'll make sure it's only a hand job next time."

Aidan laughs before he presses a kiss to the inside of Kyle's knee. "Next time? You're planning on doing it again?"

"It'll have to wait until next year, you're almost done with classes." Kyle's heart pounds, a fast, shaky rhythm at making plans that far out. "Besides, you said something about texting me instructions."

"I was just running my mouth."

"I wouldn't mind if it was more than that," Kyle says. If he was sitting in Aidan's house when his phone beeped with a detailed message of how Aidan wanted him when he came home. Maybe he'd ask for Kyle to already be kneeling. Maybe he'd want to walk into his bedroom to find Kyle on all fours, already stretched and ready for Aidan to fuck into him. Maybe—

"We can talk about it," Aidan promises. "But there's something different on the agenda tonight."

He nudges Kyle's legs apart and presses his first finger against his entrance. Kyle tips his head back against the pillows and closes his eyes. Aidan's careful with him, gentle as if they don't have regular sex, as if Kyle's body doesn't open easily for him these days.

"You can go faster, I can take it."

"I could, and you can, but you wanted slow. You asked me to take my time."

Kyle cracks his eyes open to glare. "Yeah, once your dick is in me."

"Such a way with words." Aidan grins as he works a second finger in. "I think you'll need three fingers before you're ready."

"I think your dick isn't that big."

Aidan laughs but isn't goaded into going any faster. "Can you blame me for wanting to take my time?" He rubs his thumb against Kyle's rim and Kyle spreads his legs wider, asking for more. "You respond so beautifully to me."

Kyle blushes, heat rising in his cheeks before spreading down his chest until his skin is tinged pink. He wants to hide, but there's nowhere to go with Aidan between his legs, Kyle pinned in place by Aidan's fingers and his gaze. Kyle's open and exposed, and he asked for this.

His flush depends. He should've asked for something else. A rough fuck against the wall or a look through Aidan's toy box to see if there's something in there they haven't played with before. This is going to be too much.

Something is building; between the jokes and the smiles, there's something more serious happening. He asked for gentle and careful, for Aidan to draw this out, and that's exactly what he'll do. This is like their early scene, the first-date one that left him feeling off the next day.

Or, it would be, if they didn't have months of foundation built. Then, Kyle had dropped because the next day, the scene had felt fake. It slid over his skin, oily and not right, clogging up his head and his feelings until he was down too deep to pull himself out. They had role-played a scene, but there are no personas here.

It's just Aidan and Kyle and maybe this *is* a bad idea, fragile feelings and soft touches, but they aren't fake. Aidan means every second of it, and Kyle wants him to mean it tomorrow and the day after and the one after that.

"You're quiet," Aidan says as he draws his fingers out, three now. Kyle hadn't even noticed. "You're never this quiet."

He fits a pillow under Kyle's hips to raise them, but he doesn't do anything after that. He waits, expecting an answer for a question he didn't even ask.

"I'm good. This is what I want."

And it is. This is exactly what he wants, Aidan slowly sinking into him, his cock bare so Kyle can feel every inch of it as it fills him. He locks his ankles behind Aidan's back, pulling him forward until Aidan leans in, mouth hovering over his. Aidan's fingers lace through Kyle's and hold his hands against the bed, not pinning him, just looking for those points of contact.

Kyle leans up to close the distance between their mouths, to kiss Aidan before he says something he'll regret.

Their kiss is slow and unhurried, matching the rhythm of Aidan's hips. He fills Kyle without ever leaving him, not fucking him so much as reminding Kyle that the two of them are here together.

Kyle moans into the kiss and tries to get more, tries to pull promises from him that Aidan might not be ready to give. When Aidan asked Kyle what he wanted he should've said *you*. He should've laid his cards on the table to see Aidan's reaction.

But he's a coward, too afraid to lose what he has to ask for more.

So instead he asked for this—Aidan holding his hands and kissing him, heat building between them with each gentle roll of Aidan's hips.

It's not a pace he can bear forever. Eventually, he'll need more, but for now, he holds Aidan's hands tighter and takes what he can have.

Chapter Eight

AIDAN PREPARES FOR finals and Kyle boards a plane for Madison, Wisconsin. He has a middle seat, sandwiched between Jenny and a businessman whose tie is knotted too tight. He frowns when Jenny slips past to reach her seat, his critical gaze lingering on her tattoos and the line of piercings down her left ear.

Kyle "accidentally" knocks his knee into the man's on his way by.

"Sorry," Kyle says.

The man glares at him and takes up the whole armrest between them.

"It's going to be a long flight," Kyle says.

"Are you already pining?" Jenny pulls a small fleece blanket out of her carry-on to drape over her legs. "I don't know whether you're cute or pathetic."

He thinks about making Jenny switch seats with him so she can deal with someone crowding into her space. The man bangs his briefcase against Kyle's shins which is probably deserved. He scowls. He better not end up with bruises from some asshole on an airplane.

He's supposed to be mark-free for the Expo which meant Aidan's been careful this past week not to leave any kind of impression on Kyle's skin. There are no scratch marks, no hickeys, no reminders for him to take to Wisconsin with him. And now this guy with his briefcase which is supposed to be under his seat is going to mark-up Kyle's skin.

"I'm not pining," Kyle snaps.

Jenny arches her eyebrows. "Have you told him you love him yet?"

He plucks the inflight magazine out of the pocket in front of him. It's the *In Case of Emergency* brochure which doesn't provide a good distraction, so he covers his face with it.

"I'm going to take that as a no." Jenny pats his knee. "We'll get you drunk at the bar this weekend and you can Skype your man and tell him how you feel."

Kyle lowers the brochure enough to glare. "I'm not telling him I love him for the first time when I'm drunk. I have *some* standards."

"But no courage."

"I hate you."

"That would hurt if you actually meant it."

The businessman takes a pair of headphones out of his bag and pointedly sticks them in his ears. His briefcase knocks against Kyle's shin *again*.

Kyle takes a deep breath.

THEY HAVE THEIR own rooms for the weekend, and Kyle drops his bags on the bed and then takes a shower. He washes away the travel, lingering under the hot spray until he hears Jenny pound on their shared door.

He finishes quickly after that and pulls on a pair of pants before opening the adjoining door as he dries his chest off.

"Dinner?" Jenny asks. "A bunch of people are meeting at a place down the road. You'll have to put a shirt on."

Kyle leaves the door open as he heads over to his suitcase. He rubs his towel through his hair until it's mostly dry.

"I hate hotel showers," Jenny says as she flops down on his bed.

Kyle catches his suitcase before it tips off the bed. "How formal?"

Jenny scoffs, so he pulls a long-sleeve T-shirt out of his bag. There's no one he needs to impress here. He pulls a sweatshirt over it but not before Jenny notices his shirt and kicks him.

"That's not your alma mater."

"Whatever."

He's wearing a sweatshirt. It's no one's business if he wants to wear one of Aidan's shirts while he's here. It's not the same as wearing his cuffs, but it's something.

"You have it so bad."

Kyle shrugs, agreeing without having to admit it out loud. He fusses with his hair until Jenny grows bored waiting and drags him out of the room. He has enough time to stuff his wallet in one pocket and his keycard in another before she pushes him out of the door.

They get outside, and it finally feels like spring. There's a light breeze, but Kyle probably could've left his sweatshirt back in the hotel. The ground's damp with fresh rain, but the sky is clear of clouds now. It almost makes him regret that he'll be inside all weekend.

A long table in the back is already packed full of people when they arrive. He recognizes a few faces from last year, but it's Jenny who knows people. Outside of a favor for Jenny or a demo for the club, bondage isn't his thing. He doesn't know the experts in the field or keep up with all the new books like Jenny does.

It's easy to blend into the background as she hugs old friends and meets new people. Tomorrow, he'll be on stage for people to admire, the center of attention. Tonight, he can relax.

"I'm Nikki," the woman next to him says. Her long hair hangs over her shoulder and pools in her lap.

"I'm Kyle. Nice to meet you."

"What are you here for?"

"Modeling. I'm here as a favor for a friend." He nods toward Jenny, on the far side of the table, laughing and pulling someone in for a hug.

"I heard she's doing a couple photography classes. I might try to slip into one of them. So you're here as her friend? Or her *friend*?"

"Friend," he answers firmly. "I'll model for her sometimes, but we don't do anything beyond that."

"So I might be able to get a private session?"

"If you're looking for some pictures to take home, you have a chance. But if you're looking for more, then she has someone and they're exclusive."

Nikki sighs. "That's how it always goes." She turns her attention back to Kyle and stares for a moment before she says, "Wait, I know you. You did the spiderweb shoot."

Kyle grins as he remembers that day. Jenny had strung up a spiderweb and then wrapped him in purple rope and woven it through the web until it looked like he was trapped. It had been his thank you to her for helping him with Project: Notice Me.

"I'm sorry." Nikki ducks her head, a blush rising on her cheeks. "This is my first time on this side of the convention."

"I wouldn't be here if I didn't like being noticed."

"You enjoy being the star of the show?"

"Yeah. Which always makes this a good weekend for me. Are you working with anyone in particular?"

"Randy. He's the one on the far end of the table in the backward baseball cap."

She waves to him and he waves back, smiling as he notices Kyle watching.

"He braids different materials into my hair then creates patterns from there. He calls it natural bondage."

"I'll have to check out a session."

He can appreciate the artistry in framing someone with rope or hemp or silk even if he's never found anything particularly erotic about it. Framing someone with their own hair sounds interesting but like more work than he wants to put into his fun. Even Jenny has a hard time keeping him still long enough for some of her more elaborate designs.

He saves the seat next to him for Jenny which she takes as soon as the appetizers arrive. The basket of mozzarella sticks appears then, a moment later, Jenny drops into the seat next to him.

"I swear you have some kind of sensor or something," he says.

"Something." She plucks a mozzarella stick for herself and takes a giant bite before she waves at Nikki.

"Chew and swallow before you talk," Kyle says. "For some reason, Nikki thinks you're cool. You don't want to ruin your image in the first minute."

"You swallow," Jenny mutters.

Kyle raises his eyebrows and laughs as she lunges at him, trying to cover his mouth with her hand. He holds her back long enough to say, "I *do* swallow."

Jenny groans. "I hate you."

"You gave me the perfect setup. Though, for honesty's sake, I shouldn't say that I always swallow. Sometimes—"

She shoves a mozzarella stick in his mouth which means she must really want him to shut up because she hates sharing.

Nikki looks between them, amused. "Not to get in the middle of this, but making him deep-throat a mozzarella stick probably isn't the best way to stop the blowjob jokes."

"I like you," Kyle says. He chews his mouthful of fried cheese and hands the other half to Jenny because he doesn't actually like mozzarella sticks. Those French fries loaded with cheese and bacon on the other hand... He nudges Nikki. "Want to swipe me that plate?"

"Remember, you're modeling for me this weekend," Jenny says.

"I'll go to the gym in the morning. Nikki's here with Randy, do you know him?"

"Randy's awesome. He showed me around at my first Expo. I didn't realize he was still recruiting. You'll have to tell me what panels you're on."

Introduction made, Jenny's off and running, so Kyle leans out of the women's way and eats his fries.

KYLE TAKES A walk after dinner, going a few blocks until he circles back to the hotel. He turns his computer on and changes into his pajamas while waiting. Skype pops up as soon as his computer loads, and he grins at the green bubble which means Aidan's on and waiting for him.

He hits the call button and then stretches out on his bed.

Aidan answers with a pen between his teeth and a pair of glasses resting dangerously low on his nose which means Kyle's interrupted grading. He'd feel bad about it, but his mind is stuck on Aidan in *glasses*. How has this never come up before? This seems like incredibly important information to share.

"Um," Kyle finally says.

Aidan takes the pen out of his mouth so he can smile. "Hello to you too. Is there something on my face?" He touches his cheeks as a joke, and his fingers brush his glasses. "Oh." He starts to take them off, but Kyle shakes his head.

"Leave them on. Unless it makes you cross-eyed or something."

"They're fine." Aidan shuffles his papers out of Kyle's view. "Usually you're trying to take my clothes *off*."

"Glasses don't count."

Aidan's cheeks flush as he pushes his glasses up his nose. Even through the Skype connection, his eyes are dark blue, and Kyle's distracted again. He wonders what the chances are that he'll be able to convince Aidan to wear his glasses more often. Honestly, he's surprised Aidan hasn't worn them before. He's all about the professor chic: khakis, argyle socks, and tweed jackets with elbow pads. Glasses seem to fit the look perfectly.

Is he self-conscious about them?

He doesn't need to be, and if he wants Kyle to tell him how good he looks in his glasses, then he can definitely manage that.

"How was dinner?" Aidan asks.

"It was good. The bacon cheese fries were amazing. The salad was so-so."

"Me and my pot pie are jealous."

"I thought I left you enough food to last you the weekend."

"I'll heat up the lasagna for dinner. I didn't eat lunch until four, so I'm not hungry yet."

Kyle shakes his head. "I haven't even been gone a day and you're not taking care of yourself."

"A couple days of frozen dinners won't kill me. You can stay here the week after you come home and fuss all you want."

"Better be careful what you offer. I'll take you up on it."

Aidan smiles at him as if he doesn't mind.

"I didn't mean to interrupt you," Kyle says. He wants to talk to Aidan, but if he's working, then Kyle will be fine on his own. "I can hang up. Or I brought a book. I can read while you grade."

"It's about time for a break anyway. What're you wearing?"

Kyle grins. "So it's going to be one of those video calls, is it? I'm in a white T-shirt and my pajama bottoms." He snaps the waistband. "Nothing underneath them."

"Tease. Take your shirt off."

He grabs the collar of his shirt and pulls it over his head, no fuss as he tosses it over the side of the bed. Aidan would've said if he wanted a show; besides, Kyle prefers his stripteases interactive. He likes Aidan's hands on his waist and how they slide up with each inch of skin Kyle reveals as he peels his shirt off. He likes it just as much when it's Aidan stripping him, as slow as he can, because the wait winds both of them up.

Kyle skims his hand down his chest but pauses as he reaches his pajama pants. "Now what?"

"You're easy tonight."

He's always easy for Aidan. Kyle lifts one shoulder in a shrug. "What're you going to do about it?"

"I'm not going to do anything. You'll have to do the work tonight."

"What am I going to do then?"

"You're going to jerk off for me, but your pajama pants stay on. I don't want to see your cock."

"Tease," Kyle grumbles. He reaches over the side of his bed for his bag so he can grab the lube. Once he has it, he pauses and seeks Aidan's gaze through the computer screen.

"Do you need me to talk you through it?" Aidan asks.

He doesn't *need* him to. Kyle's jerked off enough to know what he likes. If they were home, then Kyle wouldn't want Aidan's voice in his ear, telling him exactly what to do, but they're not home. He won't have Aidan's hands on him, won't even have the full weight of Aidan's gaze, but he can have Aidan's words.

"Will you?"

Normally, Kyle's the talker, because he likes the sound of his own voice and how the right combination of words can make someone desperate for him.

"Squeeze a little lube onto your hand, enough that it won't be dry but no more than that. I don't want you to make a mess. You're going to sleep in these pants."

His eyes flutter shut, already imagining it. He'll sign off Skype, close his computer, and then fall asleep in clothes that remind him of Aidan and what they just did. It won't be as good as falling asleep next to each other, but it'll be enough. He'll drift off in pants that smell of sex and carry the evidence of how good they are together even when they're not in the same place.

"Open your eyes," Aidan says. "I want to see everything I do to you tonight."

He immediately opens his eyes. Under Aidan's watch, he flicks open the cap on the lube. He tips his hand to show Aidan how much he's squeezed into his hand. "Is this good?"

Aidan lifts his eyebrows. Kyle doesn't often like being micromanaged to this degree. When they scene, Aidan is the one who gives the orders, but they've discussed what they want beforehand, and Kyle still has a fair amount of control. He can obviously stop the scene whenever he wants, but Aidan also hears what he says even if he doesn't always listen.

Tonight, Kyle wants Aidan to control everything.

"That's good," Aidan says. "Slip your hand under the waistband of your pants and slide your palm against your cock. Be careful, though. If I see your cock, then we're done."

"I have a pretty dick," Kyle points out. He obeys anyway, slicking himself up slowly so he doesn't even let the tip peek out of his waistband.

"Maybe tomorrow I'll let you show it to me."

"If I show you mine then you'll show me yours?"

Aidan laughs. "You can stroke yourself now. I want you to take your time because we aren't in a rush."

He slides his fist up and down his cock, feeling it harden under the sedate strokes. His skin is warm from being nestled in his pajamas, and it makes him wish he was flexible enough to touch his cheek to his own cock.

"Will you let me suck you when I come home?"

"You landed today. You still have a whole weekend before you fly out."

"A whole weekend away and I'm still thinking about you."

Aidan flushes and fiddles with his glasses as if he can hide his reaction. "Slide your hand lower. Cup your balls, gently."

"Look at you, being sweet to me." Kyle smiles and then rolls his balls between his fingers with a lighter touch than he usually goes for. His arousal continues to build, slow and steady, the kind of heat which makes him restless, because it isn't enough. It simmers under his skin, and he wants more. He's tempted to scrape his nails down his chest or pinch his thigh, to give himself a spark of *something*, but Aidan didn't tell him he could.

He meets Aidan's gaze evenly through the computer screen and doesn't try to hide any of his thoughts. It's dangerous to open himself up this much, but he trusts Aidan with his body; it isn't much harder to trust him with his feelings.

"Use your other hand now too," Aidan says. "Drag your thumb across your hipbone."

He does, shivers dancing down his spine at the touch. This was another reason he wanted Aidan directing him tonight. He knows how to make himself feel good, where he likes a barely-there touch and where he wants something firmer. He knows when he wants the pinch of his nails or the sweep of his fingers. And right now, it's obvious that Aidan knows all these things as well.

"I—" Kyle's voice is squeezed out of his throat. He sounds wrecked even though they've barely even done anything. "Can I close my eyes?"

"Of course. Do you need to stop?"

Kyle shakes his head. He doesn't need to stop. He wants to close his eyes and bask in this moment as long as he can.

Aidan lets him.

He continues to direct Kyle, telling him where to touch himself and how. He skims his fingers over his chest at Aidan's command. He touches his cheeks and then brushes his fingertips over his lips until they buzz. He trails his fingers down to the hollow of his throat and lower. He thinks about Aidan's fingers tracing the same path or the gentle kisses he'd lay against Kyle's skin if he was here.

He comes with his hand on his cock and Aidan's voice in his ear. Slumping against the headboard, he keeps his eyes closed. Once he opens them, he won't be able to hold on to the illusion that Aidan's here with him.

"Did you fall asleep on me?"

"M'here," Kyle mumbles. He forces his eyes open. "That was good."

"You did all the work."

"You did. All I had to do is what you told me. I like how well you know me."

"Go wash your hands." Aidan's cheeks are pink and he brushes the back of his hands over them as if he can wipe the blush away. "Brush your teeth too; anything you need to do before bed."

Kyle swings his legs over the bed before he pauses. "You're staying on, right?"

"I'm not going anywhere."

Kyle nods and heads into the bathroom. When he emerges, Aidan's lost his glasses. It's disappointing, but as he opens his mouth to protest, he's caught off guard by a giant yawn. He covers it as he slides back into bed.

"Can I do something for you?"

"I'm good."

Kyle's frown wrinkles his forehead. Usually, the only times Aidan doesn't come is when he's done something wrong. He'll retreat to the bathroom or a different room to deny Kyle the opportunity to make him come or even see it happen.

Doubt eats away at Kyle's post-orgasm haze. He sits up straighter, losing his relaxed slouch. "Did I do something wrong?"

"You were perfect," Aidan promises. "You were exactly what I wanted. Can you get under your blankets for me?"

"I'm not cold," he says even as he wiggles under his blankets.

"You will be."

Another thing Aidan knows about him. He runs warm during sex then likes to cling to that warmth as long as possible. At home, he'll tuck himself against Aidan's side. Here, he'll have to make do with layers. He wraps himself up in the comforter and then drops his head back to his pillow. He looks up at the computer screen and feels a wave of fondness for the man watching him.

"Hi," he says.

Aidan smiles. "Hi."

"Will you stay on until I fall asleep?"

"Of course. Would you like me to talk to you?"

"You don't have to. I just want to see you when I open my eyes."

"If your eyes are open then you aren't doing a very good job sleeping."

Kyle smiles but doesn't answer. He closes his eyes and pulls his blankets up to his chin. He only opens his eyes once to make sure that Aidan's still there.

He's sitting on his couch, his glasses back on. He taps his pen against his lips as he reads the papers in front of him.

Comforted, Kyle closes his eyes again.

Chapter Nine

KYLE STARTS HIS day down in the hotel gym. He woke up calm and jittery at the same time. Last night had been everything he wanted but isn't sure he's allowed to ask for. He's filled with deep satisfaction, and at the same time, he's worried it won't last.

But since it's far too early for him to be thinking like this, he changes into shorts and a T-shirt and tries to outrun his brain on a treadmill that's seen better days. At least it works, unlike the treadmill next to it.

By the time he's finished his run, done a short weight circuit, and an even longer core circuit, his shirt is plastered to his back with sweat.

He takes his time stretching because he doesn't want to be tight later today when Jenny twists and contorts his body into the positions she prefers. He sits on his mat and stretches his legs out in front of them before reaching to touch his toes.

He's moved into a butterfly stretch, his knees almost touching the floor, when he gets company. The guy who walks in has to duck so he doesn't hit his head on the doorway. He's wearing a sleeveless shirt that shows off dark skin and muscles Kyle's low key envious of.

"Good morning," Kyle greets.

The guy looks over at Kyle, assessing him the same way Kyle just had. He grins, flashing bright white teeth. "Morning."

"The treadmill on the left doesn't work."

"Thanks."

Kyle shifts into a split, breathing deep as his groin muscles stretch and his body does what he wants it to do. His legs are flat against the floor and he tips forward until his forehead rests against his yoga mat.

He counts to thirty as the whir of the treadmill fills his ears. He does his complete set of stretches and then, after checking his watch, does them again. He still has at least an hour before Jenny drags himself out of bed. If he doesn't want to eat breakfast alone, then he needs to find a way to keep busy.

After his third set, his entire shirt is a shade darker and sticks to his skin. His body hums with satisfaction, a little shaky from exertion, but nothing a hot shower and meal won't fix. He finishes his water bottle before he stands on shaky legs.

"Props to you, man," the guy on the treadmill says. He doesn't break his stride as he talks. "I know I should stretch, but I don't have the patience for it."

"Being flexible comes in handy."

The guy laughs, deep and rich, and jabs the stop button on the treadmill. "Are you here for the Expo?"

Kyle nods as he wipes his mat down.

"Me too. Do you want to grab breakfast? My partner will kill me if I wake her up this early."

"I need to shower first, but breakfast sounds good. I'd let you use my shower, but I don't have anything for you to wear. You're on the tall side."

"That's one way to put it. I'm Malcolm."

"Kyle."

They shake hands, Kyle's dwarfed in Malcolm's grip, but Malcolm doesn't try to crush his hand. They take the elevator after only a small hesitation on Kyle's part.

"I just ran four miles," Malcolm says. "I don't have a problem with the elevator."

"Good." Kyle leans against the cool wall and closes his eyes until the elevator dings to tell them they're on the fourth floor. There's no one else in the hallway, still too early for most of the hotel's occupants.

"I didn't expect to see anyone else awake this time in the morning," Malcolm says.

"We took it easy last night." Kyle slides his keycard into the door. "And I knew I was going to spend most of the day cooped up. I wanted to get a good workout in."

He pushes the door open and drops his keycard on his dresser. His water bottle goes next to it and then he tosses the remote to Malcolm, figuring he can watch TV while Kyle showers. It's a quick shower, because as soon as he's done, they can track down breakfast. His stomach rumbles its approval, and he lingers only one last moment under the spray.

He rubs a towel through his hair until it's somewhat dry and sticking up in every direction. He grins at his reflection before he pulls on a pair of lounge pants and a loose T-shirt.

Malcolm's watching the weather channel when Kyle emerges from the bathroom.

"No storms in the forecast in case you were hoping to get snowed in here."

"Definitely not," Kyle says.

"You cool if we don't eat at the hotel? They always judge me for how many eggs I eat."

"As long as we're back before lunch, we can go wherever you want."

Malcolm flashes another brilliant smile. "I saw a Denny's on the way in."

Kyle raises his eyebrows.

"Don't judge. The people at Denny's have seen some shit. Me asking for a plate of scrambled eggs doesn't even crack the top twenty of weird customers."

"You're the boss."

"Only when it comes to food. What about you?"

"Oh, I'm definitely in charge of the food. I had to rescue my partner from microwave dinners."

Malcolm looks horrified.

"I *know*."

THE DENNY'S IS a short walk away, but it's far enough that Kyle wishes he thought to grab a snack for the trip. By the time they're seated, he's ravenous. He opens the menu and the problem is that all of it looks good.

Fortunately, there's an option for that.

"Are you presenting?" Kyle asks.

"Bree, my partner is. On overcoming height differences. She'll drag me into a couple of her sessions."

"I didn't see you at dinner last night, and I definitely wouldn't have missed you."

"Being half a foot taller than everyone in the room does make me stand out, but we came in this morning. I couldn't get yesterday off work."

The waitress comes by to take their order. Kyle's settled on the French toast, scrambled eggs, bacon, sausage, and hash browns because he couldn't decide on just one thing. As he promised, Malcolm orders an entire plate of scrambled eggs in addition to pancakes, fruit, yogurt, and a double order of bacon.

Between the two of them, they make quick work of their food.

"Perfect," Malcolm says, patting his stomach. "How long do we have to wait until lunch?"

Kyle laughs and pulls out his wallet.

WHEN THEY REACH the hotel, they part ways, Malcolm to shower and Kyle to find Jenny. She's already set up in the vendors' room when he reaches her. The large room is full of tables with books stacked on them or tri-fold displays showing pictures or advertising their websites.

Jenny has her books spread across her table and extras in boxes underneath it in case she sells a lot of them. The display behind her has individual prints to sell. Some of them are photographs of him, and Kyle's drawn to those ones.

He's always surprised at how peaceful he appears when she photographs him. He looks as if there's nowhere else in the world he'd rather be. Is this what he looks like when Aidan has him? It explains the way Aidan looks at him sometimes, soft as if he's afraid of shattering him and gentle as if Kyle's someone precious.

"Vanity is a sin," Jenny tells him after he's been staring too long.

"So's half the shit I do. I don't let it stop me."

"Are you here to keep me company?"

Jenny's in black leggings and black boots that she props up on the table. Her tunic top is loose enough to slip off one shoulder, showing a hint of the tattoos curling around her arms and down her back.

"Of course." Two of Jenny's books are collections of erotic photography and the third is a how-to book that's a mix of bondage and memoir. "You should write another when you and Charlotte get married. You can call it *Tying the Knot*."

He drops into the empty seat next to her and grins. Jenny rolls her eyes, but she smiles, even if it doesn't quite reach her eyes. He knows that Charlotte's parents still won't invite Jenny to family dinner. Bringing up marriage was probably a bad idea. But if Charlotte's been with Jenny this long despite her parents' disapproval then there's no reason to think she'll stop.

"That's a stupid name."

"It's brilliant." Then the fact that she didn't argue the actual point hits him. He stops fiddling with her books. "You're thinking about it?"

"Is this one of the times where we're talking about you under the guise of talking about me?"

"Like I'm ever that subtle. I was genuinely curious, but if you don't want to talk about it, then we won't."

"Where were you this morning? I didn't see you at breakfast."

That's a no on talking about it, then. That's fine. There are plenty of things Kyle doesn't want to talk about with her even though they're best friends. Feelings are tricky, especially when he wants something so much he's afraid to name it. And he's only known Aidan for a few months. Jenny's known Charlotte for *years*.

He wants to reach out and hold her hand, offer some measure of comfort, but he knows she won't take it. So instead, he allows her to change the subject. "I made a friend at the gym and we went to Denny's."

"You do remember you're taken, right?"

"Not that kind of friend. I'm sure you'll see him this weekend, he's hard to miss. His name's Malcolm. He's here with his partner, Bree."

"Oh, yeah, I know Bree. She's a firecracker. You'll like her. I don't think I've met Malcolm before."

"He can eat a whole plate of eggs."

"Of course you'd think that's impressive."

Kyle shrugs. He's about to defend Malcolm, and his friendship criteria, when a group of three approach the table. They try to nudge each other to be the first in line, and Kyle has to hide his smile behind his hand. He was a first-timer once, but he went for bluster and bravado over shy and demure. Things haven't changed much since then except now false confidence has given way to the real thing.

"Heya," Jenny says with a friendly smile.

"Hi." It's the woman who steps forward. She even manages to meet Jenny's gaze for a fraction of a second before she stares at the table. "Are you Jenny?"

"That's me. Everything on this table was written or photographed by me. Do you see anything you like?"

The guy in the back shoves his hands so deep into his pockets that he pulls his pants down far enough to flash the waistband of his Calvin Klein boxers. His eyes dart from Kyle to one of the prints and then back to Kyle. A question builds in his gaze, but Kyle isn't sure he has the courage to ask it.

"I think this one is their favorite," Kyle says. He points to himself. It's a shoot he remembers vividly, how Jenny took her time to bind him kneeling on the bed even though all her camera work was done close-up. The shot printed here in black-and-white was her favorite of the bunch, capturing the long line of his throat as he tipped his head back, eyes closed as if he could stay there for hours.

She fussed over the knots and the layering of the rope around his wrists even though she never took a full body shot. She ended up redoing his bindings twice because she wouldn't even lift her camera until she was satisfied with her work.

There's barely a hint of rope on the photograph itself, but it's one of her most popular.

The guy who was staring blushes and drops his eyes as if he's been caught doing something he shouldn't.

"I'm a fan of that one too," Kyle says.

"You're such a fucking tool," Jenny tells him.

"Is that you?" the guy finally asks.

"You look so peaceful," the woman says. There's a note of longing in her voice. "I always think I'll feel that way, but I never do."

Her mouth twists, unhappy as if she thinks her body's betrayed her. Kyle doesn't have the best relationship with bondage, and he doesn't want her to leave this weekend thinking there's something wrong with her for not looking like Kyle does in this picture whenever she scenes.

"That picture is 75 percent Jenny being my friend and 25 percent her photography skills." Kyle eyes the picture before amending his opinion to, "Forty percent photography skills."

The woman looks surprised, but she takes a step closer to Kyle. "Really?"

"I don't let anyone else tie me up and there are some days that even though I trust Jenny with my life, I can't settle enough to be a good model. That's not my fault or her fault. It just is. I imagine it's even more complicated when you're on the pleasure side of things."

He glances at Jenny who jumps into the conversation. "My partner and I have been together for five years and there are some days where it just doesn't work. It isn't because she doesn't love me or trust me. It's because it's not a good time. If you're not finding the right headspace, then it might be the wrong time or the wrong partner. You might think you trust someone, but your body knows better than your brain sometimes. And it takes time. Kyle and I had to build to where we are."

The woman shuffles closer to Jenny's side of the table. "How do you know if you need time or to walk away?"

Knowing Jenny has the conversation firmly in hand, Kyle turns to her two friends. "Is this your first time at the Expo?"

"Is it that obvious?" asks the one on the right. His Expo badge says his name is Ray. The one on the left who had stared at Kyle's picture is Freddie.

"A little bit obvious." He smiles so they don't think it's an insult. "The first time is always overwhelming. Everything is new and a little terrifying, and you leave feeling like you didn't pay enough attention. That feeling will fade as you learn what you like and narrow your focus."

"My girlfriend wants me to tie her up," Ray confesses. "I'm afraid I'll do it wrong and hurt her. I tried to look stuff up online, but it was all about permanent damage and shit."

"So we came here to talk to real people," Freddie says. His gaze drifts to Kyle's photograph again. "I thought it would be different. Sexier, I guess."

"There's plenty of that around here," Kyle says. He opens one of Jenny's books and flips it until he finds a print of a woman on her back, her knees pulled up to her chest, her ankles bound to her wrists so her body is on display. "Is this more what you were expecting?"

Freddie blushes and nods.

"Like I said, plenty of that around here if it's what you're looking for."

"That's, uh, a lot," Ray says.

"It's definitely on the more advanced side of things. Not just the rope work. It takes a lot of trust to make yourself vulnerable like that."

He grabs a copy of Jenny's how-to book and flips to the second chapter. There's a photo of Kyle's wrists bound together in flimsy scarves. It's in black-and-white except for the shimmering green of the scarves.

"This is a good way to start. One tug and my wrists would be free. There are plenty of slip knots if you like the look of rope better. I know people who only use slip knots because for them the appeal of bondage is that their partner *could* break free but doesn't. There's nothing wrong with wherever you fall on the spectrum."

Ray traces the green scarves and then the long line of Kyle's arms. "This doesn't look too scary."

"You said you don't like bondage for the sake of bondage," Freddie says. "Why do you like it then? If that's not too personal."

"I like the attention. I model for Jenny because I know she'll put me on display. We're actually a good team because she can show off her rope skills and I can show off my body and then we both go home with other people."

"Huh."

Ray nudges his friend. "You think I should try scarves?"

Freddie shrugs. "Every time I see colored scarves, I think of when they tried to teach us how to juggle in gym class. That would kill my boner, but I don't know about you."

"Well, *now* that's all I'll be able to think about."

Kyle grins as the two friends begin to bicker.

This weekend always finds ways to be fun.

JENNY DOESN'T USE scarves in her first session of the day.

Instead, she instructs Kyle strip down to his boxer briefs and puts him on his knees on a stage in front of a room full of attendees. She talks about lighting and props and the importance of having enough time to do a shoot twice over in case things don't go perfectly the first time.

She walks back and forth as she speaks, but she'll pause at his side to run her hand through her hair. Sometimes she'll even tip his head back so she can check in with him. She's good about staying nearby when they work together. He likes the assurance that she's here and not leaving even though he knows she never would.

She's never given him a reason not to trust her, but there's always the voice in the back of his head that whispers *but what if this is the time she does?* Some days, the voice is louder than others. It's quiet today, the way it always is when he's in a room full of people.

Jenny tugs on his hair, pulling him back into the present. He flashes her a quick, grateful smile before he leans his head against her jean-clad leg.

Once she's done with her introduction speech, the real fun begins. The two of them talked through positions before this weekend but not concepts. So while he knew he'd be on his knees and eventually his arms would be bound and raised above his head, he didn't expect the giant picture frame her assistants roll out.

"Nerd," Kyle mutters as the gilded frame is secured to the floor.

There's a padded plank of wood for Kyle to kneel on within the frame and, looking up, he can see the hooks the rope will be run through.

"But a clever nerd." Jenny smiles and ruffles his hair. "We're making art come alive."

Kyle pretends to vomit.

She tugs on his earlobe before turning her mic back on so she can address the crowd. "I'll start with his torso. It will minimize the amount of time his arms will be above his head. I'll talk you through my process and take a few pictures before you can come up for your turn. We'll play with different light sources and different angles and at the end of the session, each of you will have something to take home and remember this weekend by."

Kyle kneels in the center of the frame and keeps his eyes open even as his mind wanders. He wonders how many of the people here will print out the pictures they take of him. How many of them will save the pictures to their phones to look at when they need a spark of something? How many will forget, only to stumble upon the picture weeks later and think *oh* as his picture pops up.

He'll be a part of all these people's lives. They'll think about him even if he'll never know when or for how long. He smiles as he stretches, loosening his muscles before he settles.

"Show-off," Jenny says as he trails a hand over his shoulders. Her mic is still on, but her words are for him and no one else.

He tips his head back to follow her as she goes to her rope chest so that she can pick the first material she wants to work with.

THERE'S A MIXER tonight to give attendees and presenters to mingle in a more casual setting, but Kyle doesn't have any interest in attending.

He lounges in Jenny's bed while she gets ready and then retreats to his own room.

Aidan answers Kyle's Skype call in the same glasses he wore last night, but there are no papers or pens in sight. Which means he's wearing them because Kyle likes them. He can't keep the smile off his face as he props himself up on his elbows.

"What nice glasses you have," Kyle says.

"All the better to see you with."

"Is that what you want?" Kyle asks. "Do you want to see me?"

Despite the question and all the places Aidan's answer could take them, Kyle doesn't so much as reach for the hem of his shirt.

"I can see you just fine. How was your day?"

"It was good. I made a friend. We met in the gym then had breakfast together. We're doing the same tomorrow, because his partner doesn't like early mornings, and he isn't very good at being quiet. How was your day?"

"Full of grading, but I'm almost done then I'm free for the whole summer."

"What do you even do with that much time off?"

"Get ready for next year." Aidan laughs and pushes his glasses up so he can rub his eyes. "I usually do a bit of traveling, visit my family, tweak my curriculum. I should work on my book."

"You're writing a book?"

How didn't Kyle know this? *Because I haven't known him for very long. It only seems that way sometimes.* He wonders what other things he doesn't know about him.

"It's a thing professors do. They write a book in their field, publish it, then force their students to buy it and boost their sales."

"You don't sound too thrilled about it."

"I don't feel as if I'm writing anything original. Nobody wants another book on the religious influences on classical art. If I was writing something I was invested in, then I'd be more motivated. Sorry." Aidan looks away. "You didn't call to listen to me complain."

"I called to talk to you. If you need to complain, then I'll listen. Does it make me a bad person to say I'm glad you have something to work on this summer? I'm not sure I'd get anything done if you didn't have anything to do. We can work side by side."

"I don't think either of us will get much done that way."

Kyle shrugs one shoulder, refusing to acknowledge that Aidan's right even though he probably is.

"What else did you do today?" Aidan asks.

Kyle shakes his head. He knows everything he did today, he was there for it. "I want to hear more about yours. What's the worst sentence a student's written so far?"

Aidan groans. "I'm only allowed to pick one? It's like they think I can't tell when they wrote their paper in a deadline-induced panic the night before. Okay, stay there, I need to grab my grading folder because there have been some gems this time around."

Kyle smiles as Aidan moves out of the laptop screen. He changes into his pajamas and is back in bed before Aidan returns. He puts his laptop on the bedside table and stretches out, making himself comfortable.

He doesn't plan on going anywhere else for the rest of the night.

THE NEXT MORNING, Kyle and Malcolm work out again, but this time, Jenny and Bree join them for breakfast. Bree towers over Kyle in four-inch heels, but she's still short compared to Malcolm. It means that between the two of them and Jenny sporting heeled boots, Kyle is the shortest one in the group.

"We missed you last night," Malcolm says as they settle into a booth.

"He certainly didn't miss *us*." Bree grins as she kicks Kyle under the table. "Jenny says you had a hot date."

"It wasn't like that."

"No?" Jenny asks. "You snuck away to Skype Aidan and you talked?"

Kyle flushes, blood rushing to his face without his permission.

"You *did*," Jenny realizes. "You ditched a party to talk?"

"Shut up. He had a long day."

Never mind that Kyle could've pushed for something and chose not to. He was in stitches by the end of Aidan's read-aloud, and he woke up this morning as happy as he had yesterday morning. Their relationship is founded on sex, but it doesn't mean that's the only thing there. He enjoys spending time with Aidan. That isn't something he's ashamed of.

"All those feelings you're trying to ignore? You're not doing a very good job of it."

"I'm not ignoring them," Kyle says. He knows perfectly well how he feels. "I'm just not declaring them to Aidan."

"You Skyped your man from a kink convention and talked," Malcolm says. "I'm pretty sure he knows how you feel."

Hope flutters in Kyle's chest, but it's quickly dashed by a sick twist of fear. What if Aidan *does* know? He hasn't said anything about it. Does that mean he doesn't feel the same way? Or maybe he's afraid to spook Kyle. Is he waiting for Kyle to bring it up first?

"Ugh," Kyle says.

"What'd you even talk about?" Jenny asks.

"He finished grading his finals, so we talked about the worst ones. Then we talked about our summer plans. We're leaning toward a week at his place and then a week back at mine, alternating until the school year starts again."

"At which point you two are moving in together and inviting me to the housewarming, right?" Malcolm asks.

Kyle shrugs. The future still seems too risky to think about. What if he builds up all these plans only to watch them crumble? It's best to take things one day at a time. "Our six months are up in August. I'm going to tell him how I feel and either we'll stay together or we won't."

"Kyle's in l-o-v-e," Jenny whispers, spelling out the last word.

"I can hear you. And I can spell." Kyle rolls his eyes. "How come we aren't talking about any of you?"

"Everyone else at this table has their shit together," Bree tells him.

"So do I." He huffs at the incredulous looks he receives. "I have three guaranteed months with Aidan, and I plan to make the most of them. After that, we're going to talk like adults and figure out where we go next."

"That sounds very grown up." Jenny sounds surprised. She presses the back of her hand to his forehead. "You don't have a fever."

"Hilarious."

The teasing smile slips from Jenny's face. She bumps her shoulder against his. "Aidan's been good for you. And I know I haven't known him long, but I'm sure you've been good for him."

"I think it's time to talk about you," Kyle decides. He's been on the spot for long enough. "How's your lady love?"

"She says the apartment has been quiet while we've been gone."

"Ah, so she hopes you'll stay out here another week?"

Kyle laughs as Jenny shoves him. She almost knocks him out of the booth and into their waitress, but the woman smoothly avoids his flailing limbs. She takes their drink orders and leaves without batting an eyelash.

"I told you," Malcolm says gravely. "Denny's. They've seen some shit."

Kyle just laughs harder.

Chapter Ten

THE FLIGHT HOME stretches longer than the flight to Madison did. Even without an asshole businessman next to him, it feels as if it drags too long. The weekend had been fun, but he's ready to be home.

Four times while they were on the plane, Jenny had to put her hand on his bouncing knee to make him settle. The fucking baby across the aisle did a better job keeping still than he did.

When they reach baggage claim, it's Aidan, not Charlotte waiting for them there.

"I won the coin toss," Aidan says.

"I already know she took an extra shift at work," Jenny tells him.

Kyle ignores their conversation and pulls Aidan in for a tight hug. It's too tight, but Kyle can't make himself let go. They talked every night, and even video chatted, but none of that is the same as feeling Aidan, solid and *here*, underneath his hands.

"Hi," Kyle finally says when he steps back.

Aidan looks surprised as if he didn't expect such a strong reaction. "Hi."

Jenny heaves their bags off the belt and shoves Kyle's into his chest. He grunts but doesn't drop it. He slings the strap over his shoulder and then holds his hand out to Aidan. The man smiles as he clasps Kyle's hand. He even squeezes once, a second hello. Jenny huffs and leads them through the airport and the parking lot since neither of them is paying enough attention to navigate.

"Both hands on the wheel," she orders when they reach Aidan's car.

"We don't hold hands and drive," Kyle tells her. Sometimes, he puts his hand on Aidan's knee, the way his mom and stepdad did growing up. They probably won't do that today, not with Jenny's sharp gaze on them.

There's nothing wrong with it, but Kyle already feels too exposed. She knows him well enough to know what all the little gestures mean. He doesn't want to be interrogated all over again and certainly not with Aidan in the car.

Jenny slides into the backseat and makes sure to kick the back of Kyle's seat as she makes herself comfortable. He'd complain but knows it would only encourage her.

"Did you have a good trip?" Aidan asks as he pulls out of his parking spot.

He and Kyle have talked every day, so the question isn't for him. He sits on his hands so he isn't tempted to touch and looks out the window. He only needs to be patient for a little while longer. As soon as they drop Jenny off, he can touch as much as he wants.

"The Expo is one of my favorite times of the year," Jenny answers. "I sold some books which is good, but I talked to a lot of people, which was even better. New kids just starting out and vets and other people in the field. I have so many things I want to try, I don't even know where to start."

"Like what?"

"I want to do an ivy shoot. I have this green hemp that I can use, and with a few fake flowers I think it could look beautiful."

"Does this mean I'm a crumbling building being overrun by plant life?" Kyle asks. He's used to the way Jenny's imagination runs wild after the Expo. It's a mix of finding herself in a creative environment and being surrounded by her craft, but she's always bursting with ideas after it. A lot of them never see the light of day, but he thinks this one might stick.

"You're a beautiful building, standing strong even after the apocalypse."

Kyle flips her off, but she just laughs.

"If you're not interested or unavailable then I might try to work something out with Nikki. Have you seen her hair? It's beautiful. I could weave flowers into it or even rope. I could…"

She runs away with her ideas, talking herself into as many as she talks herself out of. Kyle doesn't need to do anything but rest his head against the window and listen, her excitement bringing a smile to his face.

She talks about models she met at the Expo and general outlines of people and even brings Kyle up a few times. Neither Kyle nor Aidan says anything, but he almost wants to. When they first began, Aidan wanted them exclusive. It made sense; they were figuring each other out and it's easiest to do that when it's only the two of them.

And Kyle doesn't want to open their relationship up to other people, but he does want to return to some of the things he did before Aidan. He would model for Jenny and he'd help out at the club, doing demos or even working with less experienced Doms. He might have to stay away from the latter, but there's no reason he can't work with Jenny again or even help out around Enchanting Encounters.

He and Aidan are solid now. None of that would threaten their relationship. In Kyle's opinion, at least. He and Aidan haven't really talked about it since the beginning. He'll have to bring it up again. They can do some kind of mentorship together so neither of them feels left out. Or the two of them could demo.

He finds the second one harder to believe, Aidan doesn't enjoy attention the way Kyle does. He certainly enjoys Kyle's full attention, but he doesn't thrive on having an audience. He'll still float the idea.

Not tonight, though.

Tonight is just for the two of them.

He folds his hands tightly in his lap to keep them to himself.

THEY PULL INTO Kyle and Jenny's apartment complex and as soon as the car is parked, Jenny pops out of it with a quick *thank you* before she heads up to her apartment. Is Charlotte back from the library by now? Or is Jenny in a rush so she can unpack and surprise her girlfriend at work. Kyle, fortunately, doesn't need to go far to find his partner.

They're finally alone, and Kyle slants Aidan a look. "So..." Kyle says. "Your place or mine?"

Aidan laughs and shakes his head. "We're already at yours."

"Good choice." He's tired of waiting. He leans in for a kiss, his lips brushing Aidan's. It's soft and too short, but it will hold him over until they're upstairs and he can kiss him for real. He has no idea how he made it through Aidan's entire spring break trip when this weekend has felt unbearably long.

He sneaks a look at Aidan, trying to evaluate whether he feels the same way. He knows he has a tendency to throw himself completely into relationships. Often times, it's too much, too fast, but he can't help it. He feels what he feels. It's about finding the person who can match him, maybe not at the beginning, but given time.

He knows he fits with Aidan better than anyone else he's ever been with. And he thinks it's mutual, but he's been blindsided before. His conversation with Jenny at the Expo haunts him as they head up to his apartment.

There's only so long he can turn his own thoughts and worries over in his head before they begin to affect him. One question, and he could put those worries to rest. Or he could get confirmation for them.

He drops his duffel next to his door because it's too much effort to carry it into his bedroom. He uses his energy to grab Aidan's jacket and pull him close enough to kiss. He can't bring himself to let go long enough to slip his hands up Aidan's shirt or run his hands through the man's hair.

It's desperate, but Aidan pushes him up against the wall, pinning him there as if he's afraid Kyle will disappear.

"Missed you," Kyle says when he finally pulls back. He ducks his head as he speaks and jumbles the words together.

Aidan tips Kyle's chin up. "Me too. Did you have as good a time as Jenny?"

"Eh."

Kyle thinks about staying here, pressed against the wall, but his stomach rumbles. For some reason, planes always make him hungry. He's not sure he has anything in his apartment, but he doesn't want to go out. His plans for the day include eating something quickly and then curling up on the couch with Aidan for the rest of the afternoon.

"It wasn't bad," Kyle says as he moves into the kitchen. "But it's more Jenny's thing than mine."

He rummages through his cabinets and his emergency stash of canned goods. He pulls down some chicken noodle soup.

"Soup?" Aidan asks, having followed him into the kitchen. "From a *can*?" He reaches around Kyle to put a hand against his forehead.

Kyle laughs and bats his hand away. "I'm fine, just hungry and lazy."

"I can make grilled cheese." It's Aidan's turn to go through the cabinet. He pulls down a can of tomato soup. "This was my snow day lunch when I was younger. As soon as there was enough snow for them to cancel school, I'd play outside until I was frozen through. Then it was time for soup and sandwiches and a hot bath."

There's no snow on the ground, but Kyle could go for all those things right now. "That sounds perfect unless you have other plans."

"My turn to show off." Aidan grins and drops a kiss on Kyle's forehead before tracking down the bread.

They almost burn the sandwiches when they get caught up kissing again. They laugh and eat sandwiches that are too crunchy, dipping them in soup that's too hot. They end up skipping the bath because Kyle doesn't have the patience to wait for it to fill up.

Instead, they change into their pajamas and slip into bed.

Kyle stretches out on his side and reaches out to brush his fingers over Aidan's face. "I'm glad to be home."

It's not everything he wants to say, but it's close enough.

Aidan smiles at him, soft and fond, and he leans in for a kiss. It's not the words Kyle wanted to hear, but he kisses back and hopes this is an instance of actions speaking just as loud as words.

LIKE THE PAST two mornings, Kyle starts this one in the gym. When he gets back to his apartment, Aidan's awake too and has coffee brewing. There's a carton of eggs on the counter, but the stovetop isn't on, and Aidan looks relieved when he sees Kyle.

"I thought about scrambling eggs, but I think I used up all my usefulness in the kitchen last night."

Kyle pulls his shirt up to wipe the sweat off his face. "New summer project. I'm teaching you how to cook." He takes the first cup of coffee as soon as it's done. "I'm going to drink this, shower, then I'll tackle breakfast." He takes his first sip of coffee and hums. "Do you want to join me in the shower?"

"Are you saying I smell?" Aidan takes an exaggerated sniff of his underarm.

Kyle laughs as he leans against the counter. "I'm saying I want you naked with me."

Aidan laughs along and holds his hand out for Kyle's coffee. "Shower, food and then store? I have this end of the year thing tomorrow night. I want to pick up cookies or something."

"We can make cookies." Kyle hands his coffee over. "If I'm invited, I mean. Well, either way, we can bake but—"

"You're definitely invited. Ritchie gave me a whole list of requests."

So Ritchie wants me there? What about you? Another question he isn't brave enough to voice. He accepts his coffee back. "What about you? What's on your list?"

"I was going to buy cookies and throw them on a plate to make it look like I baked them. Anything you want to do will be a step up from that. But if you have work to get done, then you don't have to."

But what do you want? For a man who has made a career out of words, he doesn't say as much as Kyle wishes he would. But he knows something Aidan definitely wants. He finishes his coffee and offers a smile. "Shower?"

Aidan points to the coffee machine. "I'll meet you in there."

"I'll make sure to shower slowly then."

Aidan likes to savor his coffee when he has the chance, and Kyle won't rush him on his first day of vacation. Instead, he retreats back to the room on his own. He tosses his sweaty clothes in the hamper and then turns the shower on.

He scrubs off the sweat from his workout and washes his hair. He's just standing under the hot water when Aidan pulls the shower curtain back. His hair plasters to his head as soon as he steps under the spray. It takes some maneuvering so they both fit, and Kyle's reminded of why he doesn't do joint showers as soon as he leans in to kiss Aidan.

He ends up with a mouthful of water and they break apart, laughing.

"I guess the kissing will have to wait," Kyle says.

"I'm confident we'll find a way to fit it into our schedule. Any suggestions?"

Kyle's already washed his hair, but he squeezes a dollop of shampoo into his palm for Aidan. He notices and tips his head back, closing his eyes as the water rains down on his face.

"Between drying off and putting our clothes on?" Kyle rubs the shampoo into Aidan's hair, giving him an impromptu scalp massage. He relaxes under the care, so Kyle keeps going, long after the water's washed all the suds from his hair. "Then again between scrambling eggs and eating them?"

"While the cookies are in the oven?" Aidan asks. "If this is the plan then we should make something that takes longer to bake."

Kyle laughs as he picks up the body wash. "If we pick up bananas at the store then I can make banana bread. That takes at least forty-five minutes in the oven."

He takes his time lathering Aidan up, sliding his palms up and down his slick skin. It's rare that Aidan's completely naked and even rarer that Kyle isn't limited in how he can look or touch. He understands it's part of the power play and one of the easiest ways to make him desperate, but it means he could linger in the shower for hours.

He circles Aidan's wrists and then touches his long fingers. He palms his chest and the softer skin around his stomach. He kneels, careful of the slippery surface, and runs his hands up and down Aidan's legs. Aidan acts as a shield against the water, the spray hitting his back and running down, protecting Kyle down here.

Aidan extends a hand, offering him help back to his feet, and they finish showering quickly after that. They towel off, Kyle rubbing his towel through Aidan's hair until it's a mess. He laughs even as Aidan exacts his own revenge. They both look like they stuck a fork in an electrical socket by the time they're dry, and Kyle's mouth aches from laughing so much.

"Did you pencil in getting dressed?" Kyle asks.

"They'll kick us out of the store if we don't so we should probably add it."

Holding Aidan's hand, Kyle draws him into the bedroom where he leaves him by his overnight bag while he figures out what he's going to wear. Something comfortable? One of his tighter pairs of jeans? He glances over his shoulder and catches Aidan staring at him. He winks and grabs his weekend jeans. He doesn't need help getting Aidan to pay attention to him. Not anymore.

He tugs a T-shirt on next, and he's almost to the door when Aidan catches his wrist and reels him in until they're standing chest to chest.

"I was promised a kiss between drying off and getting dressed," Aidan says.

They're so close Kyle feels the words spoken against his cheek. He sways forward, bringing them even closer, and presses a chase, closed-mouth kiss to Aidan's lips. "There," he whispers.

He steps back and Aidan tightens his grip on his hand before letting him go. "Eggs."

"Then another kiss." Kyle smiles then, with more self-control than he knew he possessed, leaves Aidan standing, alone and naked, in his bedroom.

He hums to himself as he pulls out the eggs and milk. He's plating the eggs when Aidan wanders in, and Kyle points to the nearest barstool. If Aidan comes over to "help," then breakfast will burn.

Once it's done, though, Kyle drags a second stool closer until they're practically sitting on top of each other. If they didn't have plans for the day Kyle would be tempted to ask Aidan to feed him, to slip deep into a headspace where he doesn't have to worry about anything. He could place every decision made today into Aidan's more than capable hands and just exist.

Not today, though. They have too many things to do.

At the store, Kyle keeps one hand clamped around their list and the other shoved into his pocket. It helps him keep his hands to himself, but Aidan doesn't show similar restraint. He'll bump their shoulders together or brush the back of his hand against Kyle's hip and, when that isn't distracting enough, he allows his gaze to linger.

It sets something simmering under his skin. It's a restless need that, instead of being soothed with each touch, only winds him up more. By the time they're home, Kyle's patience is gone. He sets the bags down on the counter, careful of the eggs, and then pushes Aidan up against the refrigerator.

He shoves Aidan's shirt up and splays his hands against as much skin as he can. He buries his face in Aidan's neck as Aidan slides his hands into Kyle's back pockets to pull him even closer.

It's a mutual feeling then, this need to be touching.

"I'm glad to be home with you," Kyle says.

With every confession, he gets closer to what he's really trying to say. He presses a kiss to Aidan's pulse to feel the steady beat of his heart. Feeling brave, he glances up, hoping to see something in Aidan's expression or for the man to say something back.

But maybe Kyle needs to take this step too. There are a dozen ways he can say it, but before he can even find one of them, Aidan kisses him, stealing the thoughts from his head. As soon as they begin to kiss, he remembers how much he wanted to do this at the store and at breakfast and early this morning before he slipped out for the gym.

He runs his hands up and down Aidan's sides, the touch firm enough that it won't tickle. Aidan squeezes his ass through his jeans and grinds their hips together. It's frantic, rubbing against each other as their hands and mouths take everything they can.

Kyle hisses when Aidan bites at him harder than he expected and Aidan gasps when Kyle's nails scrape down his skin. Neither of them backs off, though. If anything, they cling harder, taking more and more until, finally, Aidan breaks their kiss.

He breathes heavily and rests his head on Kyle's shoulder. They're both hard in their pants, a tight, coiled tension in Kyle's body that needs some kind of release.

"Baking," Aidan says.

If Aidan's thing wasn't tomorrow, then Kyle would say *screw baking* and go back to kissing. As it is, he squeezes Aidan's sides one last time before he forces himself to take a step back. It means he has enough distance to look and Aidan's a mess; his hair wild, his cheeks flushed, and his lips a shade darker than usual from all the kissing.

Kyle has to turn his back to avoid the temptation of kissing him again. "Will you get my computer for me? It should still be in my duffel. I think it's by the door."

Usually, Kyle can bake without a recipe, but he doesn't trust himself today. He'll be distracted by Aidan and put in too much salt or not enough sugar. He collects the mixing bowls and measuring cups he'll need, and he mostly has himself under control by the time Aidan returns.

He sets his laptop down away from the mixing bowls so he won't end up with flour on the keys. He pulls up the recipe with Aidan's chin hooked over his shoulder.

"You're very distracting," Kyle says, but he doesn't elbow him to give himself more room. Instead, he increases the font size until he'll be able to read the recipe from a distance.

"Sorry." Aidan doesn't sound a least bit sorry. He grins against Kyle's neck and then presses a kiss to the underside of his jaw. "Now that the Expo is over, can I leave marks on you?"

Always.

What about something more permanent?

"Yes but nowhere visible. We're going to your work party tomorrow."

Aidan nips at Kyle's jaw again. "How do you feel about turtlenecks?"

Kyle laughs and gently pushes Aidan's face away. "It's May. No turtlenecks."

They make a mess of the kitchen, but Kyle succeeds in putting six loaves of banana bread in the oven. As soon as he sets the timer, Aidan grabs his hand and pulls him into the living room.

"I don't deserve a bed?" Kyle asks, pouting, even as he allows Aidan to push him down onto the couch.

"If I get you in bed then we're not leaving." Aidan straddles Kyle's lap, pinning him against the couch.

Kyle tugs at Aidan's shirt and he obligingly pulls it over his head and tosses it on the floor. They manage to get Kyle's shirt off too before they're kissing again. By the time the timer goes off, they're both short of breath.

Kyle taps Aidan's thigh. "I need to get up."

He doesn't want to move, he's comfortable here, and Aidan's currently sucking an impressive hickey just under Kyle's collar bone.

"Five more minutes," Aidan says.

Kyle laughs. It turns to a groan when Aidan uses his teeth in retribution.

"It's not like an alarm. If we hit snooze, then the bread will burn." He squirms as Aidan drags his tongue over his sensitive skin. "Let me take the bread out then you can keep doing this."

Aidan sighs but he tips off Kyle's lap, landing in an ungraceful sprawl on the couch. Kyle laughs and heads into the kitchen. He sticks a knife in the tallest loaf and when it comes out clean, he puts each pan on the cooling rack. He turns off the oven and then touches his fingers to the mark on his neck.

It's low enough that almost all his shirts will cover it. He's tempted to wear a V-neck anyway. Usually, Aidan leaves marks on his hips or the inside of his thighs, places no one else will see them. He *wants* to show them off. He wants to strut into the club and have a drink, dance with some friends, and know that everyone who sees him will know he's with Aidan.

He slides his hand up until he's circling his neck. *Maybe*, he thinks and returns to the couch. It's his turn to straddle Aidan. He scratches his nails lightly down Aidan's chest. He arches into the touch, pressing himself into it. The faint red lines left behind say *I was here* and Kyle dips his head to kiss down each one.

"The rest of my afternoon is free," Kyle says when he's done. "Any idea what I can do with it?"

"I have a few." Aidan smiles, his eyes crinkling the way they do when he's truly happy. "But I believe you wanted a bed."

Kyle slides off Aidan's lap and holds a hand out to him. "You promised once I was in it, you wouldn't let me leave."

"You won't want to."

Kyle darts in for a kiss and then slips away, daring Aidan to chase him.

He does.

Chapter Eleven

KYLE PICKS HIS favorite button-down to wear to the party. It's cranberry with a light sheen that catches even the dimmest of lighting. He wears a V-neck undershirt and leaves the first two buttons of the shirt undone because the collar gapes enough to show off Aidan's mark. He'll do up the buttons before they leave, but until they do, he likes the way Aidan stares.

He slices and plates the banana bread and then fusses with the cookies on the disposable platter he bought at the store.

He smirks when he catches Aidan looking again.

"Tease," Aidan accuses. He's in one of his professor sweaters. The sleeves are too long and the collar is stretched out from repeated wearing. There aren't elbow patches on this one which is a small mercy. Even better, he isn't wearing the khakis that Kyle hates.

"Tease?" Kyle echoes. "I'm just appreciating what you gave me."

"I'm not sure you'll appreciate what I'm going to give you tonight." Aidan wraps an arm around Kyle's waist and pulls him close.

Kyle's smirk only grows. He cups his hand over Aidan's cock. "I think I will."

"Brat."

"You like me anyway."

Aidan catches Kyle's wrist and uses his hold to walk Kyle backward until he bumps up against the pantry. "I do, but that doesn't mean I won't punish you for your backtalk." He leans in until he can whisper in Kyle's ear. "Maybe I won't fuck you when we get home."

Kyle's cockiness wavers. It's one thing goading Aidan into spanking him which, to be fair, isn't an effective punishment if he wants it. Aidan knows how to actually punish him, and he wants to avoid that.

"Let me make it up to you?" Kyle asks.

Aidan gives him a small smile and lets go of his wrist so he can pull his sweater sleeve back and check his watch.

Kyle behaves himself, keeping his hands at his sides and not touching.

"We should go if we don't want to be late."

Kyle's already thinking about the reusable grocery bags he has and which one he should pack their desserts into. He's wiggling out from where Aidan has him pinned when a single look makes him freeze. Aidan's expression is dark and wanting, edged with something that makes Kyle hold himself completely still. He feels like prey except he doesn't want to hide. He wants to see how exactly Aidan plans to take him apart.

It's mixed signals because Aidan just said they need to leave, but he looks at Kyle as if he's about to start something.

Aidan leans in, and Kyle's lips tingle in anticipation of a kiss. Instead, he deftly does up the two top buttons on Kyle's shirt before he steps back. "There." His gaze lingers as if he can still see his mark through Kyle's shirt. "Now we can go."

"Kiss me first?" Kyle asks.

Aidan grins and Kyle's stomach swoops with arousal then frustration, because he knows that expression. It means good things but no right away.

Sure enough, Aidan says, "I want you thinking about it all night." He leans in again, close enough for Kyle to kiss him if he was allowed to. "I like it when you're desperate."

"*Now* who's the tease?"

THE PARTY IS held in one of the campus dining halls. There are four long tables set up with desserts and drinks and the occasional Crockpot on them. The rest of the room is open so people can mingle.

There's a lot of people.

Kyle's never put much thought into how many faculty and staff work at a college, but the answer is an overwhelming number. The room isn't packed full, but there isn't as much open space as he thought there would be. It's a mix of casual and more formal dress. His outfit falls somewhere in the middle which means he won't stand out either way.

"I should've made more banana bread."

They pass by a cluster of people who already have plates piled high with brownies and cheese cubes and meatballs.

"You're fine," Aidan promises.

Kyle discreetly shuffles closer to Aidan, but he wasn't as subtle as he thought, because Aidan drapes an arm around his waist and pulls him even closer.

"Better?"

Kyle nods. He's not sure why he's so uneasy. He likes people. He's good with them. This is just...a lot. These are all the people Aidan works with, and Kyle wants to make a good impression. Even more than that, he wants to reflect well on Aidan. But being back in a college makes him feel like at any moment someone's going to ask him how far he can recite pi or if he's done tomorrow's reading yet.

"I *liked* school," Kyle mutters as he sets the banana bread and the cookies on a free spot on one of the tables. He has handwritten cards with full ingredient lists in case anyone has any allergies, and he props those up next to the plates. "I didn't even take math in college."

"Did you say something?" Aidan stops peering down the table to look over at Kyle.

"Nothing important." Kyle folds up his bag. "I'm going to run this out to the car."

"Do you want me to come with you?"

There's someone headed their way, a woman in business slacks and a floral print top who waves to Aidan to catch his attention.

"I'll only be a minute."

He heads back the way they came as the woman asks Aidan if he's recovered from finals yet. He's out of earshot by the time Aidan answers, too much noise in the room for Aidan's voice to carry.

It's warmer outside than it was inside, and Kyle tugs at his collar as he crosses the parking lot to where his car is. He throws the bag in the trunk for the next time he goes to the store and takes a deep breath. Meeting Aidan's colleagues is a good thing. It means they're growing more involved in each other's lives and the more involved they are, the more likely they'll stay together.

"You can do this," he tells his reflection. He'll smile, make some small talk, and eat a bunch of junk food. This is basically the perfect afternoon, and it'll end with him and Aidan together. He takes another breath and then heads inside.

Either he doesn't remember where he left Aidan or Aidan's moved because he doesn't see him right away. And it turns out that looking for a guy in a sweater while in a room full of professors isn't very helpful. It's easier to spot Ritchie who is setting out clear cups of chocolate pudding with crumbled Oreos and gummy worms.

"It's dirt," Ritchie explains when Kyle wanders over to investigate. "It's not actual dirt. You can eat it. I thought it should be layered to more accurately represent soil composition, but Caroline said no."

"I am the ruiner of fun," Caroline says. She pulls Kyle in for a hug. "Where's Aidan?"

"I put something in the car and now I've lost him. I guess that means you haven't seen him yet."

"I'm sure Culvert cornered him again." Ritchie starts a new row of pudding cups. "She keeps trying to set him up with one of her children. Though, she might've moved onto her grandchildren?" Ritchie shrugs. "It won't work either way. Her kids are too old for him and her grandchildren are too young."

"Huh."

"It won't work for other reasons," Caroline says.

Ritchie looks up, confused. Caroline sighs and looks pointedly at Kyle.

"Oh, right." Ritchie nods. "You don't need to worry. She talks up her daughters and granddaughters at every function and hasn't had any success yet."

"I know Aidan's a catch." Kyle eyes the chocolate-covered pretzels to his left and wishes he had a plate so he could start filling it with snacks. "I'm not surprised other people have noticed."

Ritchie stops fussing with his plastic cups. Even Caroline stares at him.

"I was expecting more fireworks," Ritchie says.

"I don't do the jealousy thing." To his right is a fruit platter and there are toothpicks, so Kyle spears a piece of honeydew. "Either my partner and I like each other enough to be together or we don't and we find people we like better."

"He does like you," Caroline says.

"A lot," Ritchie adds.

"I know." Kyle picks a piece of cantaloupe this time. He isn't worried about Aidan talking to this Culvert person and being tempted by her offspring. He and Aidan are solid. They've spent the past two days unable to be more than a couple of feet apart. That doesn't happen if Aidan's unhappy or growing bored.

"There you are." Aidan appears on Kyle's left. He hands him a plate filled with fruit, mini quiches, and chocolate-covered pretzels. "I'm sure I missed some stuff, but we can do a walkthrough together."

Aidan's plate has three slices of banana bread, and Kyle can't help his smile. "I can make that for you any time, you know."

"Like today." Aidan takes a giant bite out of his first slice as if he's afraid Kyle will try and take it from him.

"I'm glad you like it."

"Do you want some dirt?" Ritchie asks, offering Aidan a cup.

Aidan glances at Kyle as if he's looking for his recommendation.

"It isn't actually dirt," Kyle says. He pops a mini quiche into his mouth. "These are good."

"Pavel makes them and they always go fast. I wanted to make sure to grab you a few before they were gone."

If they were home, Kyle would lean in for a quick kiss. He isn't sure of the rules on that here, so he keeps it safe and bumps Aidan's shoulder with his. "What's the game plan? Fortify ourselves with food then mingle or is this your crew for the night?"

"I wish." Aidan glances around them with some of the same apprehension that Kyle felt earlier. "I should say hi to the rest of my department then some other people so I'm not accused of being too insular."

"I want to meet this infamous Culvert. I can give her some tips to pass on to her grandchildren if she really wants you to date them."

Aidan points an accusing finger at Ritchie. "Why?"

"You were missing. I figured she found you."

"Professor Culvert is the oldest professor at our college," Aidan tells Kyle. "She's a very nice woman who thinks I'm too old to be single."

"You're not single. Let's find her and tell her the good news."

"Food first. Then a drink. *Then* we can talk."

Kyle laughs and tucks himself against Aidan's side.

PROFESSOR CULVERT—"CALL me Connie"—has the best glasses Kyle's ever seen. They're gold-wire with wings on the edges. When she passes them over to Kyle to look at, he recognizes Greek letters even though he doesn't know what they mean.

"These are awesome. Can I send a picture to my friend?"

Connie eyes him, evaluating.

"Charlotte's a librarian. She'll be jealous."

Connie waves a wrinkled hand, giving permission. "Does she have a glasses collection?"

"She has a vest collection. Halloween, Winnie the Pooh week, train week. She has Clifford themed vests and a handful of Frog and Toad ones. She's embraced being a children's librarian."

"She can't be as old as me then. She wouldn't be able to sit on the floor for story time." She turns her attention to Aidan. "You like kids."

"Not enough to read to them every day. There's a reason I'm a college professor and not an elementary school teacher."

Kyle can see where this is headed even if Aidan either hasn't noticed or is ignoring it. "Charlotte's spoken for." Then, smiling, as he does it, Kyle slips an arm around Aidan's waist. "So is Aidan."

He hands Connie back her glasses, and she puts them on before squinting at the two of them. Aidan tenses as if he's afraid of her reaction, but Kyle doesn't. He can read people well, and Connie seems like the kind of woman who enjoys meddling because she wants people to be happy.

Sure enough, her face breaks into a delighted smile. "It's about damn time."

"What?" Aidan asks.

Connie shakes her head. "I've been talking your ear off about my kids for *years*, waiting to see if you'd bring someone to one of these parties just to shut me up."

"You asked me if I wanted to go to a football game with your granddaughter."

"She's far too young for you."

Kyle laughs and holds on to Aidan tighter as he tries to squirm away.

"How did you two meet?" Connie asks. She looks over at Kyle. "I assume it was all your doing. Our Aidan isn't always the most observant."

"Fortunately, I'm not very subtle." Kyle shares a smile with Aidan. "I noticed him when I was out one night and decided I wasn't going to be happy until I got him to notice me back."

"There's more to it than that. Don't try to lie to an old woman."

"I'm going to need another drink for this," Aidan says. He drops a kiss on Kyle's forehead. "Do you want anything?"

"Some of that punch that tasted like watermelon sherbet?"

"Finn from the chemistry department makes it every year," Connie tells him. "Be careful with it. It tastes like punch, but a couple drinks in and the room starts spinning."

"Half a cup," Kyle says.

"Do you want anything?" Aidan asks Connie.

"More of the banana bread if they have it."

"Kyle made it," Aidan says, pride evident in his voice.

Connie looks over at Kyle who gives her a little wave. She turns back to Aidan. "He's a keeper. Don't screw this up."

Kyle blushes as Aidan leaves, surprised that Connie's so observant and glad they're this obvious. He leads her over to one of the many tables scattered across the room and helps her sit before he sits down across from her.

"You too," Connie tells him. "Aidan's a good one."

"I know." He has a front seat to how amazing Aidan is. He's kind and funny and caring and they have great sex. He isn't looking to lose any of that.

"This does make sense now that I think about it," Connie says. "I spent all this time trying to introduce him to women and he was unfailingly polite and completely uninterested. If only I'd known I should've been introducing him to nice, young *men*."

"I'm glad you didn't."

Connie raises her eyebrows. "It's like that, is it?"

"He's a good one. You said it yourself."

"How long has he been hiding you away for?"

She peers at him through her winged glasses, and he knows what she's really asking. *Have you been together long enough to be serious? Do I need to look out for my coworker? Can I trust you with him?*

Aidan returns before Kyle can answer, holding a plate with two slices of banana bread and a full cup of punch.

"I didn't have enough hands for everything. I figured we could share."

"My mouth has to touch where yours did?" Kyle asks. "Ew." He laughs at the look Aidan gives him and pulls out the chair next to him.

"Young love," Connie says. She points a wrinkled finger at Aidan. "Now I've met Kyle, there'll be no more hiding him away. You'll bring him to every faculty function, and he'll make me banana bread for each one. Next time, you should add walnuts."

Kyle nudges Aidan's shoulder with his. "We can probably manage that."

"Yeah." Aidan doesn't quite meet Kyle's gaze, abnormally shy. He clears his throat. "We can do that."

WHEN THEY GET home, Kyle kicks his shoes off by the door. He leans against the wall and undoes the bottom button on his shirt. He catches Aidan's gaze and grins. "You're on summer break. Are you up for a late night?"

Aidan answers by pulling his sweater over his head and dropping it next to their shoes. It leaves him in a thin white undershirt. He crooks his finger and Kyle goes, unable to resist the invitation. As soon as he's in reach, Aidan catches his wrists and reels him the rest of the way in.

The kiss starts off where they left off this afternoon, heated and a little desperate. Kyle pushes forward, taking every inch Aidan gives him and then more. He tangles one hand in Aidan's hair and the other in his shirt.

It's heat and the sharp sting of teeth, then the soothing press of lips, and Kyle would be embarrassed at how quickly he gets hard except he's been waiting for this for *hours*.

But he has some standards, so he rips his mouth away from Aidan's and asks, "Bed?"

"You're very eager for someone who isn't getting my cock tonight."

Kyle's already turning toward his bedroom when he pauses. "What?"

Aidan grins and it has the dark edge that makes Kyle's stomach swoop in anticipation. The look means Aidan will twist him up until he doesn't know what to do except take what he's given and enjoy it. It promises a long night filled with frustration and a few tears and something amazing if only Kyle will let it happen.

The past two days, they've been reacquainting themselves, everything slow and gentle or rushed in a desperate sort of way. It was exactly what they needed, and he's settled enough now that he's willing to work if it's what Aidan wants. But if Aidan thinks he isn't going to argue for a good fucking, then he has another thing coming.

"I told you before we left," Aidan reminds him. He undoes the first two buttons of Kyle's shirt so he can thumb over the bruise he left earlier.

It isn't even that sensitive anymore, but Kyle groans at the light pressure and then tips his head back as Aidan presses harder. Aidan slides his hand higher until his palm rests against his Adam's apple. With every breath and bob of his throat, he feels Aidan's skin against his own. It isn't hard to breathe, but it's a reminder that Aidan's there and could make it harder.

Would he let him?

Some of his thoughts must show on his face because Aidan pulls back. "Not tonight."

"You already have plans for the night." Plans Kyle's going to have to work to change.

"I have some ideas.'"

"How flexible are they?"

Aidan laughs and swats him lightly on the ass. "I guess we'll see. Bedroom."

"Yeah, I—shit. My cuffs are in the car." Along with his overnight bag which he forgot in his rush to get inside.

"Get them then meet me in my room."

He grabs his bag and when he reaches Aidan's room, he pauses, because Aidan has his toy chest out. It's the size of a couple of shoeboxes, easy to store in his closet, and when he catches Kyle watching, he pulls out a pair of nipple clamps.

"Put your cuffs on the bed then wait for me. I want to undress you myself."

He won't argue with that part of the plan. He navigates his bag by touch alone, unwilling to look away from Aidan's casual perusal through his box. The clamps are put on the bed. The ball gag, which Kyle can't help but frown at, is put back in the bag. The thin vibrator goes on the bed. So does the wooden paddle.

Kyle adds his own offering to the collection before he drops his bag to the floor. It makes a muffled thump. "Um," he says, still staring.

"You asked if I was up for a late night," Aidan says. "This is my answer."

"It'll be a very late night if you're planning to use all of that."

Aidan hasn't put the lid back on his box yet. "Is there anything you don't want?"

He knows if he points to anything then Aidan will put it back, no questions asked. But he's also curious to see how Aidan plans to use it all. One at a time? All at once? He did say a long night. Maybe Aidan will bring him right to the edge, then test to see which of his toys will tip Kyle over.

"You can think about it," Aidan tells him. "I'm going to grab a few things from the kitchen."

He takes that as permission to touch the things Aidan's taken out and to look through the ones he left behind. He rummages through the box until he finds a cock ring. He turns it over in his hands, wondering if he should ask Aidan for it. He seems to be in a teasing mood, and Kyle will need all the help he can get if he's supposed to hold out.

"We don't need that," Aidan says.

He's returned with a bottle of water, a bottle of orange juice, and a pack of peanut butter crackers.

"And we need all this?" Kyle drops the cock ring back into the box, wondering where exactly tonight is headed.

"Do you want to know?"

And, well, if that's an option…Sometimes he wants to know what's going to happen. Listening to Aidan lay it out, offering his input, that's a kind of foreplay in and of itself. But sometimes he wants the surprise of it. As long as, "You have a plan?"

"I've been thinking about this since you went away. I've had to make some adjustments, but I know what I want."

"Surprise me then."

It's Aidan who looks surprised, caught off guard the way he is sometimes when Kyle shows how much he trusts him. It makes him want to hug the other man, to sink to his knees and close his eyes and put himself in Aidan's hands and *show* him how much he trusts him. Someone like Aidan, kind and gentle and loving, he should never doubt himself. He deserves every ounce of trust Kyle gives him.

Aidan sets the drinks and snack on the bedside table and then holds his hand out. "Watching you touch yourself for me while you were away was good, but I've been impatiently waiting to touch you myself."

Kyle's gaze darts to the toys on the bed, but he doesn't say anything, because he's already on shaky ground, and he doesn't want Aidan to take fucking him completely off the table. Even if the paddle isn't the same as Aidan bare-handed spanking him and even if the clamps aren't as good as Aidan's teeth biting into Kyle's flesh, they're both good. It's Aidan who holds the paddle and the clamps which means he's still dictating what Kyle feels and when.

He undoes the buttons of Kyle's shirt cuffs first, parting the fabric so he can lay a gentle kiss against Kyle's wrist. He does left and then right. Then he kisses the mark he left just below Kyle's collarbone. His teeth nip at the sensitive skin there, and Kyle hisses out a slow breath. The bruise won't fade if Aidan keeps this up, but he's not sure he wants it to. He likes the idea of carrying around something Aidan gave him.

It's almost the same feeling that he gets as Aidan buckles his cuffs, claiming him for the night. He stares at the soft brown leather, unable to look away as Aidan helps him take his pants and his briefs off. He's still staring once he's naked and only Aidan's fingers tipping his chin up manages to break his spell.

"Red if you want to stop," Aidan tells him. "Yellow if you need to slow down or take a break. Snap if your mouth is otherwise occupied."

Kyle nods, a shiver racing down his spine as the night grows more real. They always have a safe system set up, but the fact that Aidan's reminding him of it means he has something more intense than usual planned.

"Show me," Aidan says.

Kyle snaps with one hand and then the other.

"Good." Aidan kisses his cheek. He holds up a forearm length of chain with a clip on each end. "I would like to use this. If you want it off, then you can tell me, snap, or take it off yourself. We also don't have to use it."

He doesn't answer right away. He knows Aidan won't leave him. It's a trigger they're both aware of, and he wouldn't put through Kyle through that. He even gave him three backups in case he needs them. But fear isn't as easily dismissed as he might like it to be.

If Aidan's offering, though, it's because he has a plan, and Kyle can trust that he's factored Kyle's feelings into the plan. He won't intentionally push him past where he's comfortable.

"We can use it," Kyle says. "How do you want me?"

Aidan groans as he leans in to bring their mouths together. He kisses Kyle as if he's trying to climb inside him. He pushes Kyle backward and Kyle goes until he hits the bed. Another surge from Aidan knocks him onto the mattress, Aidan following him down. It's enough to break the kiss, so Aidan kisses his cheek and then the curve of his ear.

It tickles, and Kyle laughs and squirms a little as he tries to get away.

Aidan plants his hands on either side of Kyle and pushes up so he isn't lying on top of him. "Will you sit against the headboard for me?"

He has to wiggle to scooch backward until he's how Aidan wants him. He can't help his glance at the wooden paddle and wonders how it'll come into play if he's like this. Then he brushes the thought aside. This is Aidan's plan. All he has to do is let it happen.

He fusses with the pillows until he finds a comfortable position because he isn't sure how long Aidan will want him like this. He stretches his legs out until he can nudge Aidan's shoulder with his toes. Aidan's smile makes something warm curl in Kyle's stomach. Then Aidan lays a kiss against his ankle bone and the warm feeling spreads, anchoring itself as it goes.

"You're far away," Kyle complains.

Aidan laughs as he crawls up to straddle Kyle's waist. He holds the chain up, one last check-in. At Kyle's nod, he clips one end of the chain to Kyle's right cuff. He loops the chain through the headboard before he clips the other end to Kyle's left cuff.

It raises his arms above his head and arches his back, pushing his chest out. He would feel exposed except the way Aidan stares makes him feel displayed instead. The flush spreading across his skin only makes him even more aware that Aidan's still in his pants and a thin white T-shirt.

"Since I can't touch you, can I see you?"

"Soon."

Aidan moves them both around until he's kneeling between Kyle's legs. It means Aidan's finally taller than him. He has to dip his head for them to kiss instead of pulling Kyle down to him. Kyle smiles into the kiss.

They kiss until Kyle's eyes slip halfway shut because it's too much effort to keep them open. He falls back against the pillows because he knows Aidan will chase him, fitting their bodies together as they continue to kiss. If he didn't know that Aidan had plans for the night, then he could be happy doing this for the next hour.

But there is more in store for the night. When Aidan pulls back, Kyle meets his gaze rather than chasing him for another kiss.

"Good?" Aidan asks.

"I'm good."

Aidan rubs his thumb across Kyle's bottom lip, leaving the imprint of his touch before he moves his attention elsewhere. He ducks his head to press the flat of his tongue against Kyle's nipple. It catches him off guard, and he gasps and then jerks into the wet heat. Aidan's hands immediately grip his hips to hold him down.

It's hard to stay still as Aidan traces tight circles around his nipple, coaxing it to harden before Aidan sets his teeth against the sensitive flesh. He groans and twists his hands until he can grip the headboard the way he wants to hold on to Aidan.

His cock leaks against his stomach, twitching with each sharp sting of Aidan's teeth. It gets better, or worse, when Aidan soothes the sting with his tongue. He twists and wriggles, but there isn't anywhere for him to go.

When he's convinced even a moment longer will be too much, Aidan switches sides.

By the time Aidan pulls back, Kyle's face is red and overheated. His hair sticks to his sweaty forehead, and his hands ache from being balled into tight fists. But his entire body tingles with anticipation, wanting more even as he's afraid that he won't be able to handle it.

He catches his breath in time to lose it all on a sharp exhale when Aidan picks up the nipple clamps.

"Oh," he says. His gaze darts from the objects to Aidan's grin to the ceiling. If Aidan uses them, then his hands and mouth will be free to touch other places. It's exactly the kind of maddening tease which will test him. He wants that more desperately than he thought he would. It's an opportunity to prove himself, and if he does well enough then maybe Aidan will fuck him.

"Please," Kyle begs. He can't tug Aidan closer with his hands so he uses his legs instead, drawing his knees up until he can hook them around Aidan's body. A light slap to his thigh makes him drop his legs back against the bed.

"I hear you," Aidan promises. He brushes his knuckles across Kyle's cheek, soft and gentle, a whisper of a touch.

Then he pinches Kyle's left nipple between his fingers. It's enough of a contract to make Kyle gasp. He arches into the touch then tries to pull away. But there's nowhere to go, and Aidan waits patiently for him to figure it out. When he does, slumping against the headboard, Aidan's smile turns dark, a mean edge to it.

"Please," Kyle asks again.

Aidan attaches the first clamp. The tiny teeth dig into Kyle's skin, and he squirms as he tries to get used to the feeling. These are their lightest pair, designed to keep a steady beat of arousal pumping through his veins. He can't help but lick his lips and follow the chain connecting the first to the second, still held in Aidan's fingers.

Once he's sure he has Kyle's full attention, Aidan puts the second one on. Then, smile growing, he wraps his finger around the chain and twists until it pulls tight. It knocks the breath right out of Kyle's lungs as heat and want pulse in his dick as if there's a direct line there from his nipples.

He squirms and it pulls the chain even tighter. His dick bobs against his stomach, smearing precome everywhere it touches. His face flames even hotter, and his own breathing fills his ears, heavy and desperate and too loud.

He wants to arch forward to relieve the tension and sink back against the pillows to make it worse. Aidan makes the decision for him. He plants his free hand on Kyle's collarbone, covering the mark he left there, and nudges him back against the headboard.

For a moment, it's too much, and he's afraid he's about to split apart. But then Aidan releases the chain and Kyle slumps against the headboard, the moment broken before breaking him. He feels strangely cheated.

His nipples burn with residual pain, the sensation going straight to his balls. They're heavy, already uncomfortable, and the night's barely begun. If Aidan's already pushed him this far...

"I'm going to cry tonight, aren't I?"

"I hope so," Aidan answers, enough longing in his voice that Kyle's heart skips a beat.

If he didn't trust Aidan then the prospect would scare him, bound here as Aidan strips down all his defenses, exposing him and pushing him until he gives him everything he can. But he knows that once he's at his most vulnerable, Aidan will be at his most gentle. He'll break Kyle down and then stay by his side as he puts him back together.

Kyle tips his head up, begging for a kiss. Aidan leans in, giving Kyle this as if he knows Kyle needs the assurance. Then, once Kyle sighs into the kiss, Aidan shifts his approach. The kiss grows deeper, Aidan using his tongue to claim Kyle's mouth as thoroughly as he's claimed the rest of him. Kyle lets him.

Aidan pulls back, too soon for Kyle's liking, but when he opens his mouth to protest, Aidan slips the chain between his teeth. "Hold that."

There's enough slack in the chain that there's only a slight tug if he keeps his head bowed. As soon as he looks up at Aidan, though, the clamps pull against his nipples, the kind of pain that makes him pant around the metal in his mouth.

He ducks his head to ease the tension, and of course, that's the moment Aidan chooses to get off the bed. He tracks Aidan's movements the best he can. Then, as if he knows Kyle's range of vision, Aidan pulls his shirt over his head and takes another step back.

It means he has to choose—relief and staring at the bed, or hurting himself so he can see Aidan. He raises his head and grinds his teeth together so he doesn't lose his grip on the chain. His cock jerks as if he can come just from a couple of clamps on his nipples. He can't, though, and pleasure is followed quickly by frustration.

Aidan strips with efficiency, leaving his clothes in a pile on the floor, as he opens the bedside drawer. He pulls out the lube and a condom. Kyle's brow furrows as he tries to figure out how Aidan will fuck him when he's sitting like this. And, as much as he wants Aidan, he was told he was going to have to earn it, and he hasn't done anything yet.

His questions are all answered when Aidan joins him on the bed and instead of nudging Kyle's legs apart, he reaches between his own.

Kyle's mouth falls open, the chain slipping out, as Aidan begins to finger himself. Aidan smiles when he notices and lifts the chain. "Open."

Kyle takes the chain again.

"Good," Aidan says.

He finishes stretching himself and then rolls a condom on Kyle's cock. The firm slide of his hand is almost enough to send Kyle over the edge. He clings to his control because he doesn't want to lose the chance to feel Aidan on his cock.

Not that he thinks he'll be able to hold out for long anyway. Pain throbs in his nipples, slipping into pleasure by the time it reaches his cock. Once he has Aidan tight and hot around him, he's afraid he won't be able to help himself. He wishes he'd fought harder for the cock ring.

Aidan slicks up Kyle's cock with a teasing smile, as if he knows how torturous the touch is. Then he sinks down on him as slowly as possible. It makes his entire body coil tight, waiting for the next inch and wondering if this is what will snap his control. By the time Aidan's fully seated, tears cling to Kyle's lashes.

Aidan cups Kyle's face in his hands, smearing lube across one cheek, adding to the mess of sweat and tears. "You can come whenever you want."

Kyle shakes his head. Of course, the one time he needs Aidan to tell him to hold out is the one time he tells him he doesn't have to. If Aidan told him to wait, then he'd be able to wring more control out of himself.

Aidan kisses the corner of Kyle's mouth and flicks his tongue over the metal chain. Kyle tips his head up for a better kiss and sucks in a breath at the spark of pain as the clamps pull painfully at his nipples. His cock jerks, and Aidan groans before kissing him harder, uncaring that Kyle can't kiss him back.

As soon as Aidan stops kissing him, Kyle bows his head to give himself some relief. It means he has an up-close view of Aidan's thighs, spread over his waist. Aidan's cock curves up toward his stomach, hard and leaking, and Kyle wants to touch. When he tries to reach down, his hands are caught tight.

He pulls again as if somehow the chain will snap and he'll free himself. It doesn't get him anywhere except more frustrated.

"I'm right here," Aidan promises. He cups Kyle's cheek with one hand as he uses the other for balance and leverage as he rolls his hips. Aidan *is* here, surrounding him, holding him, and it's somehow not enough.

It's also too much. With every flex of Aidan's thighs, he clenches around Kyle's cock. He wants to come before he shatters into a thousand pieces, but he doesn't want to lose a single second of this. He tugs on his restraints again, because he doesn't know what else to do.

"You're good," Aidan tells him. "You're perfect for me. Tonight is for you. You can come whenever you want."

Not yet, just a moment more. Kyle shakes his head without thinking and almost rips the clips off his nipples. He shouts and the chain falls from his mouth. Fresh tears spring into his eyes and Aidan squeezes tight around his cock and that's all it takes.

Kyle throws his head back, a dull thunk against the headboard as his orgasm is ripped out of him, too fast, an overload of his body. It whips through him before he can even enjoy it, and it leaves him limp against the headboard as he pants for breath.

Aidan kisses him, sloppy and desperate, stealing Kyle's hard-won air right out of his mouth. He can't do much but tip his head and allow himself to be kissed. His cock spurts weakly into the condom, and his nipples ache, two sharp points of pain now there's no pleasure for them to ride along with.

"I've got you," Aidan murmurs as he pulls back. It's then Kyle realizes he's whimpering, tiny little sounds he can't help. Aidan runs a soothing hand through his hair and carefully wipes the tears from his eyes and his cheeks.

He eases himself off Kyle's cock and then unclips his wrists from their chain. He takes the condom off and disposes of it before he returns to Kyle's side.

He's hard but doesn't even seem to notice as he kneels next to Kyle. His palms roam over his stomach and sides, touching as much skin as they can until they slide upward. "Are you ready?" Aidan asks.

His fingers are scant inches from the nipple clamps. The pain has ebbed into a steady burn and taking them off will hurt all over again. It's not the kind of thing he can be ready for, but Kyle nods anyway.

Aidan takes the first clamp off. Before Kyle's even finished gasping, Aidan's mouth is there, his tongue soothing as it presses against Kyle's abused flesh. With his right hand, he reaches down to lace their fingers together, and Kyle squeezes tightly as Aidan takes off the other clamp.

Aidan lingers longer this time. He grows bold, flicking his tongue over Kyle's nipple to make him squirm. He's not sure if he likes it or not. His body is all crossed wires and mixed messages right now, waiting for someone to untangle him.

He shakes his head as Aidan smiles at him, showing off enough teeth to be a warning. But he doesn't say no and he doesn't push Aidan away. And when Aidan's teeth nip against his skin, he arches into the pain instead of trying to wriggle away from it.

Aidan cups his balls with his free hand before sliding up his cock and Kyle shakes his head again. Aidan smiles and takes pity on him, only squeezing him once before pulling back.

"How are you feeling?" Aidan asks as he takes a bottle of water off the bedside table. He unscrews the cap and pauses, waiting for Kyle's answer.

"Good." He glances at Aidan's erection. "Will you fuck me now?"

"I want you to drink some water then I want to paddle you."

And well, Kyle won't turn down either of those things. Aidan helps him sit up a little more so he won't choke when Aidan puts the bottle to his lips and tips it up. With the restraints gone, Kyle could do this himself, but he likes how Aidan cups the back of his head and coaxes him into a drinking a couple of mouthfuls of water before he takes a few long sips of his own. It makes him feel cherished, someone Aidan wants to be careful with.

Aidan holds the water out in offering.

"I'm set for now." He eyes the paddle. "How do you want me?"

"Elbows and knees."

His body is entirely too soft and too stiff in turn. His spine feels liquefied, as if he could contort himself any way he wanted. It's a colossal effort to turn himself over. Aidan's hands are there, though, holding him up, holding him *together*, as he gets himself situated.

He braces his forearms on the mattress and realizes that if he loses the position he's in, then he'll rub his chest against the sheets. "You don't want me wearing a shirt tomorrow, do you?" he accuses.

Aidan laughs, pleased with himself. He strokes Kyle's sides and his back. He palms Kyle's ass next as if he's mapping all the places he wants to strike. "Do you think I can turn your ass as red as your face?"

"You can do anything you set your mind to," Kyle says, with faux seriousness.

He's rewarded with a sharp, bare-handed slap.

"I guess I don't have to ask if you're ready," Aidan says. "You're back to sassing me." He taps the paddle against Kyle's skin, too light to mean they've started, more like a warning that they're about to start. "What do you say if you need me to slow down?"

"Yellow."

"And if you want me to stop?"

"Red."

He ruffles Kyle's hair. "I don't want you to count, let me worry about how many. All I want you to do is feel."

Kyle doesn't think that will be a problem. Sure enough, the first blow knocks all thought out of his head. He rocks forward on his arms before he braces himself better. The paddle comes down again. It doesn't hurt, not yet, but he knows where it's landed.

A few strikes later is when it hurts, a slap of pain which spreads out into a pleasant warmth. He tilts his hips up, asking for more.

"I'm not even close to done," Aidan promises.

Aidan hits him, steady as a metronome, allowing Kyle to sink into the rhythm. The pain is a heavy, dull kind which allows him to slip into his head. Instead of jolting him out of his headspace, each blow sends him deeper into it.

He doesn't know how much time has passed when Aidan finally stops, only that his shoulders shake with the effort to hold himself up. His face, chest, and ass all burn in a way that makes him feel flushed which easily translates into aroused. He looks down his body and groans when he realizes he's hard again.

Aidan's already let him come once tonight, and he's not sure he's lucky enough to be allowed to come again. Is this his punishment, forced to hold himself in check as Aidan fucks him?

He groans and slides his knees further apart, opening himself up more.

"Is that what you want?" Aidan's lips are cool against Kyle's overheated skin as he kisses the base of his spine. He kisses his way up until he's draped over Kyle's back, his mouth right by his ear. "Do you want me to slick my fingers up and fuck you the way I did to myself earlier?"

Kyle arches his back so he's touching as much of Aidan as possible. He's still greedy enough to want more. "Please. I want you to open me up then fuck me."

Aidan nips at his ear and then pulls away. He can't help his whine, feeling betrayed, even as a glance shows Aidan reaching for the lube. It's still too far away. He needs Aidan touching him again, *in* him.

Aidan palms Kyle's ass, lube momentarily forgotten. "I did a good job with you."

"Always," Kyle says. *But you're not done. Please don't be done.*

He takes his time fingering Kyle open. He stretches him with one finger then two. He doesn't move on to three until Kyle's clawing at the sheets and begging for more. He's fully hard now, cock hanging heavy and neglected between his legs.

He twists his hips, chasing Aidan's fingers, but he pulls them out. Kyle curls his hands into fists. "Please, fuck me. I need it."

"Like this?"

There's a snap of a condom and then Aidan slides the vibrator into him, too smooth and too small to pass as Aidan's cock. Kyle tosses his head, because no, this isn't what he wants. But then he remembers Aidan telling him he wasn't going to get his cock tonight. And *this* is his punishment, allowed to come but denied the only thing he truly wants.

Aidan flicks the vibrator on, and Kyle groans, the sound pulled from somewhere deep inside him. Aidan fucks him with it, hard, relentless, and after the spanking, it doesn't take long for Kyle's arms to give out on him, unable to hold himself up. Aidan hauls him up by the hair until he's on his knees, back bowed, and his head resting on Aidan's shoulders.

It shifts the vibrator inside him, and Kyle's quick to wrap his fingers around the base of his cock. Aidan releases his grip on Kyle's hair to curl his hand around the shaft of his cock. His strokes are steady and sure, and he twists his wrist the way he knows Kyle likes and laughs when Kyle's entire body trembles with the effort to hold himself in check.

"Come," Aidan tells him. "Show me what you have left."

The permission is all he needs. Aidan presses his cock flat against his belly so he spurts out against his chest, weaker this time than the first. He slumps against Aidan, trusting him to hold him up.

Aidan gently lowers him to the bed, turning him so Kyle's on his back, looking up at Aidan's half-lidded eyes.

"Beautiful," Aidan says. He rubs Kyle's come into his skin.

He doesn't take the vibrator out, though. He's too raw from his orgasm for it to feel good, and Kyle wriggles, trying to knock it out. All he does is clench around the toy which makes it even worse. Aidan turns the setting down, but he doesn't turn it off. Kyle feels as if his entire body is vibrating from his toes to his fingers to his head as his hair flutters against his forehead.

He's aware of every single part of his body all at once, and it's overwhelming. It's too much for his brain to focus on, but he can't narrow his focus into something manageable. His nipples throb from earlier, the sheets feel too rough against his ass, and his dick twitches with some misguided hope that he can grow hard again.

"I can't," Kyle says.

Aidan turns the vibrator off and then eases it out. He doesn't leave the bed this time to throw the condom away, just leaves the vibrator at the end of the bed where it won't get in their way. He keeps a hand on Kyle's thigh to ground him as he wipes new tears from Kyle's cheeks.

Still touching Kyle, he reaches for the water bottle they shared earlier. It takes more coordination this time to help Kyle drink. "Next time, I should bring a straw?"

"Next time?" Kyle asks. "Let's see if I survive this one first."

Aidan coaxes a little more water past his lips. "Does this mean you're done?"

"You have *more* planned?" His gaze catches on Aidan's cock, still hard, and guilt washes away all the lingering pleasure from his own orgasm. He's come twice and got so wrapped up in himself that he forgot about Aidan and—

"Hey," Aidan interrupts before Kyle's thoughts can spiral too far away from him. "I'm the one with the plan, remember? You've been so good for me tonight, doing exactly what I ask."

He melts with the praise and the reassurance that he hasn't done anything wrong. Still, it's unfair to leave Aidan hanging. And now Kyle's completely spent, there's nothing to distract him from Aidan's pleasure. He reaches for Aidan's cock, only for Aidan to catch his wrists and pin them, gently, against the mattress.

"You have two choices," Aidan says. "I can jerk off on your stomach then rub my come into your skin or I can fuck you."

Kyle's wanted Aidan to fuck him for *days*. It's all he could think about at the Expo when they were separated by hundreds of miles. Then he landed, and Aidan held back and teased them both. And now Kyle's finally being offered what he wants when he can't do anything about it. He can't even lift his head for a drink of water right now. Aidan's wrung him out, one of his favorite feelings except how it's the worst because he's *useless*.

"It won't be good for you," Kyle says. *I won't be good.* The thought threatens to bring with it more tears but not the fun ones this time.

Aidan runs his hands through Kyle's hair, catching his attention and holding it. He cradles his face between his hands, gentle and careful, as if he knows the wrong look or word will shatter Kyle beyond repair. "I promise you I'm not so selfless I gave you two options I wouldn't enjoy. I'm going to get off, and I'll do it while looking at you and seeing all the ways I've taken you apart tonight. If you don't want me to fuck you, then I won't, but don't say no because you think I don't want it."

He still doesn't understand how it'll be good for him, when Kyle's this exhausted, but he trusts that Aidan wouldn't offer if he didn't want it. And since Aidan's promised he won't be disappointed, the answer is easy.

"Yes."

"Yes, what?"

"Yes, I want you to fuck me."

Aidan smiles and ducks his head to kiss Kyle's cheek. "If it's too much—"

"Yellow or red, I know. Please, don't make me wait any longer."

"Because *you're* the one with reason to be impatient."

"I've been thinking about your cock in me for days. Skype sex is good but not as good as having your hands on me. I spent the whole flight wondering if I could convince you to fuck me as soon as we were home. I—what're you doing?" Kyle frowns as Aidan retrieves a condom from the bedside drawer.

"Easier cleanup. It's non-negotiable. You're going to be hurting when we're done, and I won't make it worse."

"Fine."

Aidan rolls the condom on and then slicks his cock with a generous amount of lube. Kyle still hisses out a slow breath when he slides in. He's not sure how to describe what it's like when Aidan fucks him, slowly and carefully, watching Kyle's face for any sign he wants to stop. It's not that it hurts, but it doesn't feel good either. He just *feels,* and it threatens to rise up and swallow him.

"Look at me," Aidan says, less of a demand, closer to begging.

Kyle didn't realize he'd closed his eyes. When he opens them, Aidan is there, above him and staring down. Whatever was threatening to overwhelm him backs down, replaced by Aidan's strong grip on his hips and searching gaze.

"Please," Kyle breathes. He doesn't know what he's asking for.

Aidan thrusts into him, almost too hard. Kyle grabs Aidan's wrists and holds on. He can't do anything but lie there as Aidan fucks him. His ass scrapes against the sheets and his nipples throb, his entire body marked by Aidan. There's a bite mark below his collarbone and finger marks against his hips. He's marked and owned and loved, and it's too much.

Tears well up in his eyes, and Aidan falters, concerned.

"Green," Kyle tells him because he doesn't want this to stop. Not when they're right on the edge of something good, something *important*. "Green. Please, fuck me. You promised. You—"

Aidan kisses him, hard and desperate. His thrusts grow erratic as he kisses him deeper and deeper until all Kyle feels is Aidan, in him, on him, around him. Aidan bites at his lips and his jaw. He bows his head to kiss the hickey he left earlier.

When he comes, he squeezes Kyle's hips so hard that Kyle will feel the imprint of his fingers for the next hour.

I want more, Kyle thinks, dazed as Aidan pulls back.

"You constantly amaze me," Aidan murmurs. He touches Kyle's face with reverence.

Kyle tangles a hand in Aidan's hair to pull him back down. They should probably get up, but he isn't ready for them to be apart yet. "Good, then?"

"*You* were good," Aidan says. "You were—you *are* more than I thought you'd be."

"You make me better."

"You make me better too."

Kyle smiles, sleepy but sated, *happy*. "That's the way it's supposed to be."

He tugs on Aidan's hair, gentle, and once he has Aidan's attention, he smiles. Aidan smiles back and then leans in. His lips ghost across Kyle's in the barest definition of a kiss, a thousand words tied up in a small gesture.

Chapter Twelve

IMPORTANT OCCASIONS, IN Kyle's opinion, are marked by candles. Things like birthdays and anniversaries. Declarations of intent rank up there as well. Their six months are drawing to a close, and he doesn't want to put this off any longer in case Aidan thinks Kyle doesn't want to continue what they're doing. He very much wants to continue, but without the time limit this time.

They've taken things slow, stopped and evaluated as needed, and it's time for the next step.

Hence the candles.

Unlike Aidan, Kyle owns candles appropriate for the occasion. There's no scent of pine drifting through the room. Walking into his apartment won't feel as if he's passing by a Bath & Body Works, an olfactory assault that always leaves him with a headache.

His candles are long and thin, for show rather than practicality. He likes to think they set the tone for the evening. Aidan pauses when he sees them. A small frown creases his forehead. "I already ate dinner."

"These aren't for dinner." If they were then the candles would be on the table in the kitchen instead of the coffee table in the living room. He catches Aidan's hands and tugs him over to the couch.

On the table between the two candles is a nondescript white box. Aidan's gaze is drawn to it, and Kyle picks it up.

There won't be any easing into this conversation. Not that they need it. In some ways, the past eight months have been building to this moment.

Kyle lifts the lid off the box. Nestled in a few sheets of tissue paper is a simple brown collar. He's had it for years, waiting for the right person to give it to. When Aidan unknowingly picked out a pair of matching cuffs, Kyle took it as a sign. Then he agreed to a six-month extension of their play to figure out if there was, in fact, something building between them.

Now, he holds the box in two hands, an offering. "Will you accept my collar?" He feels as if he's offering a dozen other things along with it. He holds his breath, his hopes for the future now out of his control.

Aidan drags his gaze from the collar to Kyle's face. He searches for something, and Kyle bares his thoughts and emotions for Aidan to sift through. He could say his nights with Aidan are the best he's ever had and the mornings are sweet, something he's always wanted. He could say he trusts Aidan more than he's trusted anyone before, with his body and his heart. He could even say "I love you," but the collar says all of that and more.

Aidan's fingers brush Kyle's as he grasps the box. "I would be honored," he answers, formal, but exactly what Kyle would expect from him.

A smile steals over Kyle's features, bright and blinding. His hands finally give in to their shaking, but Aidan holds the box steady. "Should we seal it with a kiss?"

It's Aidan's turn to smile, and his lips are still curved upwards when he presses them to Kyle's. It's a chaste kiss and far too brief. When Aidan pulls back, his attention is drawn to the collar again. "May I put it on you?"

"It's yours."

"It's in my care."

Kyle nods and then, finding his voice again, asks, "Please."

He sinks to his knees, the box now lifted above his head. Aidan accepts the box from him and then takes the collar out. He turns it over in his hands, touching every part of it as if he wants to imprint himself on it. Kyle wets his lips, but he doesn't need to beg, because Aidan kneels and gives him what he wants.

The collar is padded on the inside for comfort, and Aidan pulls the strap through the buckle. He fits it through a hole and Kyle says. "Tighter. Please."

"For tonight." Aidan cinches it one hole tighter.

The leather presses against his skin now as if he's being held. Every time he swallows it grows tighter. If they were scening now, something strenuous, then it might be too tight. But for kneeling on the hardwood and staring at Aidan as he's stared at in return, it's perfect.

Well, he could do without the hardwood. "Couch?" he asks.

"Bed," Aidan counters. It's an even better idea. They stand together and Kyle blows out the candles before he leads Aidan back to his bedroom.

"You're not bringing the candles with us?" Aidan teases.

"I have different ones for the bedroom."

"Not tonight," Aidan says which could be a no to wax play or a no to sex by candlelight. Either way, Kyle isn't concerned. He wants the lights on so he can stare his fill. He unbuttons his shirt, the one he put on for the occasion fifteen minutes ago and is already taking off. Like the candles, it's served its purpose. He drapes his shirt and his slacks over the back of his chair. He tosses his socks and undershirt in the laundry.

He tugs on the waistband of his briefs. "Do you want to do this?"

Aidan shakes his head. He pulls open the drawer closest to Kyle's side of the bed and takes out his cuffs. "Tonight, I only want to put things on you."

Kyle isn't about to argue with that. He steps out of his briefs, adding them to his laundry, and sits on the edge of his bed. He holds his wrists out to Aidan who carefully buckles one cuff and then the other. These he doesn't pull as tightly as if he knows that Kyle wants to sleep in them.

A wonderful thought hits him as he hooks his ankles around Aidan to keep him close. He can keep his cuffs on longer now. They've used them to mark time, in scene versus out of scene because boundaries were important to protect their feelings. They still need boundaries but different ones.

Kyle can wear his cuffs after a scene has ended without blurring scene and relationship now they're both tied firmly together. He can wake up with the reminder that this is real and his. He pulls Aidan in for a kiss, unable to keep his feelings completely to himself.

Aidan has to bend to kiss him, and it can't be good for his back. It's also too much distance between them. Kyle pulls him closer until his knees bump the bed and then he pulls him the rest of the way down. He's on his back, legs dangling over the side of the bed, and it isn't comfortable except that Aidan's now on top of him. He rucks up Aidan's shirt and breaks their kiss long enough to pull it over his head.

"A T-shirt?" Kyle asks as he tosses it on the floor.

"You didn't tell me tonight was going to be a special occasion."

He props himself up on his elbows and Aidan shifts back enough that they can look at each other without going cross-eyed. "You would've dressed up for me?"

Aidan looks at him with an expression that Kyle chooses to translate as *I would do anything for you.* He knows it's true, and it's a terrifying amount of power to have. Is this how Aidan feels whenever Kyle sinks to his knees or holds his wrists out? The possibilities swirl in his mind, everything he wants and apparently can have, and it makes him shaky and needy and desperate.

He hauls Aidan in for another kiss.

It's good until the seam of Aidan's pants catch against his cock. He winces and pushes on Aidan's shoulders until he backs off. Kyle pops the button on Aidan's pants, but he glances up before moving onto the zipper. "May I?"

Aidan nods and stands up so it's easier for Kyle to pulls down his pants. Another look and after Aidan's nod, Kyle pulls down his boxers too. It leaves him naked, coarse brown hair sprinkled over his body. His cock, half-hard, makes Kyle glance up, another question in his eyes.

"Ask me," Aidan says.

"May I suck you? Please?"

"You may."

Kyle reaches back to grab one of the pillows off the bed. He tosses it near the wall. Aidan steps back to watch as he fusses with the pillow then kneels, his bedroom wall against his back. He beckons Aidan forward and the man moves until Kyle's secure between him and the wall.

He thinks it's everything he needs until Aidan's fingers touch his collar. *Oh,* Kyle thinks, looking up. *This* is what he needs. Then he takes Aidan's dick in his mouth, eyes sliding shut, and everything settles. He doesn't move, and Aidan doesn't pressure him.

He could stay here all night if Aidan would let him, caught in this peaceful bubble. All of the urgency from earlier is gone, replaced with a steady calm. Aidan is here and the press of his collar is a constant reminder that he isn't leaving. Tears spring into his eyes, natural and nothing he allows himself to be ashamed of.

Is this what it feels like to have everything he wants?

He's grounded and content even as part of him wants to spiral up and up and up. He's afraid he'll lose himself if he isn't careful. Aidan slips a finger under his collar, pulling it even tighter and reminding him that he isn't going anywhere Aidan doesn't let him. Aidan won't let him lose himself.

He's safe.

He blinks back tears as he opens his eyes so that he can look up at Aidan. He's already looking at Kyle, a soft, fond expression on his face. It turns into a smile when he notices Kyle's paying attention.

"Hey," he says. He runs one of his hands through Kyle's hair, messing it up. The other stays around his neck, touching the collar as if he still can't believe Kyle's wearing it. If Kyle didn't feel it every time he swallowed, then he'd need to touch it too.

He pulls off Aidan's cock so he can say, "Hey," back. He kisses Aidan's hip, the knobby part that's all bone. Earlier he said he wanted to suck Aidan's cock, and he does, he always does, but mostly he wants the two of them wrapped up in each other for the whole night. He wants to be touching everywhere; here where the skin stretches thin across Aidan's hip bone and here where he's soft.

He slides his hands up Aidan's thighs. "Bed?"

"Are your knees bothering you?" Without waiting for the answer, Aidan catches Kyle's elbow and helps him to his feet.

"They're fine. I just—" Kyle waves a hand as if to say *I don't know what I want except that I want you.* Some night, he's full of plans, but tonight everything comes down to one thing. Aidan.

Aidan walks them toward the bed, his hands steady on Kyle's hips. "Do you trust me?"

He could point to the cuffs on his wrists or the collar around his neck or the fact they're in Kyle's bedroom, one of the few partners he's ever let into his space. But Aidan already knows all that. Is he looking for reassurance? If so, it's something easy for Kyle to give him. "Yes."

"Lie down on the bed," Aidan says. He grabs the pillow from the floor and fits it under Kyle's hips before taking the lube from the nightstand drawer. "Condom?"

Kyle shakes his head. He wants to feel everything tonight.

Aidan opens him up slowly, taking his time, treating Kyle as if he's something precious. He doesn't need to which is why it feels so good. He flushes as Aidan whispers praise and whines as Aidan draws his fingers out, only to sigh as he sinks them in again.

He curls his free hand around Kyle's neck, and Kyle tips his head back to give him better access. He's caught and held, secure between Aidan's hands. His pulse flutters and his thighs tremble, and he's poised on the edge of something, but he isn't in a rush to see where he goes when he tips over.

When Aidan finally fucks into him, he's as careful as he was with his fingers.

"Remember that scene we did early on, where we role-played a first date?" Kyle feels now like he did then, his chest tight as if his heart isn't big enough for all his feelings. Only, this time, he doesn't have the sour taste of *fake* ruining every moment.

They aren't acting out a scene. Every touch, every glance—they're *real*. Tomorrow morning, when Kyle wakes up, every single thing Aidan says to him tonight will still be true. "I wanted it to be true."

"What about now? Is it still what you want?" Aidan cups his cheek. "I can pick you up for dinner and take you somewhere nice. We can hold hands and order a bottle of wine, and after dessert, I can take you home and have you like this."

Back then, they skipped the dinner, picking up the scene on the walk home. This time, Kyle wants everything, but he's shy as he asks, "Are you asking me out on a date?"

Aidan's eyes twinkle with mischief. "Technically, I think it might be our first one."

"If you try and pull that chivalrous bullshit again—" Kyle's threat is cut off as Aidan laughs.

When he stops laughing, the smile stays on his face. "I'd like to take you out." He brushes his fingers over Kyle's collar. "There are a lot of things I'd like."

Ask and I'll give you them all. Kyle curls a hand around the back of Aidan's neck and draws him in to kiss him. It's a reminder that they were in the middle of something, and he keeps Aidan close as Aidan fucks him again.

They're going to go on dates, dinners and movies and walks in the park where they negotiated their first formal meet-up. They'll dress up and dress down and sometimes wear nothing at all. There will be dinners out and breakfasts at home, and he won't have to worry that he's pushing for too much or that he's falling too deeply.

They've both fallen, and they're here together now.

He reaches between them to fist his cock. He matches Aidan's pace, slow, and draws out each stroke.

"Was I taking too long?" Aidan teases.

There's no urgency tonight, and Kyle wants to make this moment last as long as possible. He also wants to fall asleep so he can wake up and do it all again tomorrow. Even for him, that's sappy, and he flushes and looks away.

Aidan wraps his hand around Kyle's so they can stroke him together. "Look at me."

Compelled, Kyle looks up at him again. There's no judgment in his face, no mocking smile lurking at the corners of his lips. "You were breathtaking the first time I saw you, up on the table for a spanking. Someone told me you'd never worked with the Dom before, and I couldn't believe it. You were trusting and giving, and I wanted you to turn that lidded gaze on me. I wanted to earn every bit of trust you so freely gave."

Aidan touches the collar again. When Kyle swallows, it presses tighter and pushes into Aidan's grip. His eyes flutter but don't close. Aidan swipes his thumb over the tip of Kyle's cock and smears the precome around the head. "You've given me more than I ever thought you would."

"You've earned all of it," Kyle promises.

His next words are lost on a gasp as Aidan strokes him again, twisting his wrist just the way Kyle likes. Where things had been slow before, they speed up now. They know each other well enough that Aidan dismantles him, quickly and efficiently, with rolls of his hips and the curl of his fingers.

Kyle weaves his fingers through Aidan's hair and tugs as he comes. Aidan pulls out and jerks himself a few times before he spills, adding to the mess on Kyle's stomach. They both breathe heavily afterward, and Kyle's limbs feel so heavy they anchor him to the bed.

"You made a mess," Kyle says.

Aidan laughs. "*We* did." He grabs a tissue off the nightstand to wipe up the worst of it. "I'll get a washcloth."

He does even better than that. He comes back with a *warm* washcloth and wipes them both down. Kyle tosses the washcloth in the laundry basket when Aidan's done.

"I could've done that," Aidan protests.

"I've seen your aim."

Aidan laughs, conceding the point. He unbuckles Kyle's collar and places it on the other nightstand. He kisses the skin it covered and then tucks his face against Kyle's neck. Kyle reaches over to turn off the light next to the bed and curls his arm around Aidan's shoulders.

"Good night," he murmurs.

Tomorrow, there will be breakfast and important discussions about what exactly the future looks like. But for tonight, he's warmed by Aidan curled around his side and the knowledge that there *is* a future for them.

About the Author

Tamryn studied English and Creative Writing in school but has been writing since she could first hold a pencil. Recently, she's turned her focus toward writing erotica. She enjoys writing stories where sex comes first, then feelings, because doing things out of order can be fun.

Other books by this author

The Daniel and Ryan series
Delayed Gratification
The Start of Something New
Who I Am When I'm With You
Positive Reinforcement
Performance Review
Spa Weekend
Weekend Getaway
Caught In Between
Testing the Limits
Tournament of Champions

The Enchanting Encounters series
To Seek and to Find
To Have and to Hold

Also Available from NineStar Press

Connect with NineStar Press

www.ninestarpress.com

www.facebook.com/ninestarpress

www.facebook.com/groups/NineStarNiche

www.twitter.com/ninestarpress

www.tumblr.com/blog/ninestarpress